VLEMK
THE BOX-PAINTER

VLEMK

THE BOX-PAINTER

By

John Gardner

ILLUSTRATED BY CATHERINE KANNER

LORD JOHN PRESS, NORTHRIDGE: 1979

VLEMK
THE BOX-PAINTER

I

THERE ONCE WAS A MAN who made pictures on boxes. Snuff boxes, jewel boxes, match boxes, cigar boxes, whatever kinds of boxes people used in that country, for keeping their treasures in or giving as presents to friends and loved ones, the people would take their boxes to this man, who was called Vlemk the box-painter — or they'd buy one of the boxes the man had made — and he would paint pictures on them. Though he was not old and stooped, though old enough by several years to grow a moustache and a beard that reached halfway down his chest, he was a master artist, as box-painters go. He could paint a tiny picture of a grandfather's clock that was so accurate in its details that people sometimes thought, listening very closely, that they could make out the noise of its ticking. He painted flowers so precisely like real ones that one would swear that they were moving just perceptibly in the breeze, and swear that, pressing one's nose to the picture, one could detect a faint suggestion of rose smell, or lilac, or foxglove.

As is sometimes the way with extremely good artists, this Vlemk the box-painter was unfortunately not all he might be when it came to matters not pertaining to his art. When he was painting, up in his bright, sunlit studio that looked down over the houses and streets of

1

the city, he was a model of industry and good sense. He kept his brushes, paints, glazes, and thinners as carefully and neatly as a fussy old widow keeps her dishes and spoons, and he worked with the deep concentration of a banker or lawyer studying his books in the hope of growing richer. But when his work was finished, whenever that might be, since sometimes he worked all night, sometimes all day, sometimes for an hour, sometimes for a week and a half without an hour out for rest —this Vlemk changed completely, so that people who had seen him at work would swear now that he was not the same person, surely not even that person's brother, but someone else entirely.

When the artist wasn't working, it was as if some kind of demon got into him. He would go to the tavern at the end of his street, where he talked very loudly and waved his arms wildly, knocking over beerpots and sometimes tipsy old men, and though many people liked him and were interested in his talk, since none of them had the knack of painting pictures as he did, sooner or later he was too much for even the most kindly and sympathetic, and they would call the police or throw him out into the alley by the collar of his shirt and the seat of his trousers. Sometimes he had dealings with unsavory characters, drunkards, pickpockets and pilferers, even a certain murderer who took his axe with him everywhere he went.

The artist was not proud of himself, needless to say. Often, sitting up in his studio high above the city he would moan and clutch his head between his hands, saying, "Woe is me! Oh, what's to become of me?" But moaning was no solution. As soon as he'd finished

his work for that day, or that week, as chance would
have it, down he would go into the city again, and his
fall to dissolution would be as shameful as before.
"What a box I'm in!" he would cry, looking up from
the gutter the next morning. It had long been his habit
to think in terms of boxes, since boxes were his joy and
occupation.

One morning when this happened — that is, as he
was crying "What a box I'm in" and struggling to get
himself up out of the gutter, where he was lying among
bottles, old papers, and the remains of a cat — a carriage
was passing, driven by a uniformed man in a top-hat.
The driver was elegant — when his boots caught the
sunlight they shone like polished onyx — and the carriage on which he sat was more elegant still, like a
splendid box of black leather and polished golden studs.
When the carriage was right alongside the poor artist, a
voice cried out, "Stop!" and at once the carriage stopped.
A small hand parted the window curtains, and a pale
white face looked out. "Driver," said the person in
the carriage, "who is that unfortunate creature in the
gutter?"

"That, I am sorry to say," said the driver, "is the
famous box-painter Vlemk."

"Vlemk, you say?" said the person in the carriage.
"Surely you're mistaken! I once visited his studio, and
I'm certain I'd know him anywhere! That creature in
the gutter is some miserable, pitiful wretch without a
talent in the world!"

"I assure you, Princess," said the carriage driver
sadly, "that the filthy thing you see in the gutter is
Vlemk the box-painter."

In horror, Vlemk covered his face with his hands and arms, for now he recognized that the person in the carriage was indeed the Princess, soon to be Queen of the Kingdom, people said, since her mother had been dead for years and her father was declining. Vlemk was so ashamed to be seen by such a person in his present condition that he fervently wished himself dead.

"Shall I throw the poor devil a coin?" asked the driver. "I assure you he can use it, for if rumor be believed he squanders all he earns by his art on his life of dissolution."

"Heavens no!" said the Princess, parting the curtains more widely in order to get a closer look at Vlemk. "What earthly good would a coin do him? He'd spend it on further debauchery!" So saying, she closed the window curtains and ordered the driver to drive off.

"Heartless monster!" cried Vlemk, clumsily rising and staggering a few steps in the direction of the swiftly departing carriage. He was so angry he raised both fists to the sky and shook them.

But secretly, Vlemk did not blame her for her words. All she'd said was true, and if he was wise, he knew, he would thank her for her righteous severity. "Woe is the Kingdom," he said to himself, "whose rulers are dismayed by every sniffle." Besides, when she'd parted the curtains wide, he'd gotten a very clear look at her face, and with the force of a knife in the back or an arrow in the chest it had struck him that the Princess was the most beautiful creature he'd ever set eyes on.

When he returned to his studio that day he found he was incapable of painting. His brushes had a malevolent will of their own, dabbing too deeply, as if angrily, into the paints, so that every stroke he made in the picture was slightly off its hit and inefficient, like the work of an amateur, so that he had to wipe it off and start over. By mid-afternoon he understood that his case was hopeless. He'd lost the will to do perfect paintings of animals or flowers or rural landscapes, paintings of the kind that had made him famous. Indeed, he'd lost the will to paint at all. Carelessly, irritably, he put away his materials, hardly noticing that the brushes were less clean than usual, the paints not well capped, one bottle of thinner tipped sideways and dripping on the floor. "What a box I'm in!" he said, but dully, without feeling.

In the tavern he discovered that nothing the establishment had to offer was exactly what he wanted. The wine, he knew without tasting it, was bitter, the beer too full of froth, the brandy too sugary and thick. "What *is* it I want?" he thought, sitting with his mouth open, hands clasped in front of his chin, eyes rolled upward, staring without interest at the cracks in the old, sagging ceiling. All of the regulars of the tavern threw puzzled, slightly irritable glances in his direction, baffled at his seeming so unlike himself. By this time, people grumbled, he should be singing, if not kicking up his heels or starting arguments. One might have thought they would be pleased, since Vlemk could be a nuisance when behaving in his normal way, but in general this was not the case. Even the laziest and most base of the regulars —not including the four mentioned earlier, who were all in some sense artists themselves— were simple people who led complicated lives, and Vlemk's disruption of what little routine they could persuade themselves they kept was distressing.

"What *is* it I want?" Vlemk asked over and over, inaudibly, sitting by himself at his table by the window.

"Why doesn't he drink?" grumbled the regulars, or all except the four. "Why doesn't he *do* something?"

The four—the barmaid and three glum men who wore their hats low and went about armed—said nothing, hardly noticing. The flaxen-haired one, formerly a poet, was fast asleep with his eyes open. The one in the glasses, an ex-violinist, was picking the pocket of the laborer just behind him. The third one only stared, like a cat before a mousehole. He was the axe-murderer.

Secretly, of course, Vlemk had known from the beginning what it was that he wanted, and when he came to full awareness of what that something was, he was filled with such misery that he could no longer stay indoors. He rose without a word to anyone, not so much as a glance at the sullen, fat barmaid, and with his hands thrust deep into the pockets of his painter's frock, which in his misery he'd neglected to leave behind in the studio, he walked to the door and, after a moment's hesitation, out onto the street.

He walked quickly, like a man with some urgent purpose, though in fact he had nowhere in particular to go and nothing much in mind. If someone had asked of him the time of day, he would have had to look around to determine that it was evening, almost nightfall. He walked from street to street and from bridge to bridge in this dejected state until, to his surprise, as the last glow of sunset was fading from the clouds, he found himself standing at the gates of the royal palace.

The Princess, as it happened, was at just that moment returning from walking her greyhounds on the palace grounds. At sight of the box-painter, the greyhounds set up a terrific rumpus and jerked fiercely at their leashes in an attempt to get at him and scare him away, with the result that the Princess was drawn, willy-nilly, to where Vlemk stood gazing in morosely at the palace door. When they reached the iron gates between Vlemk and themselves, the dogs leaped and snapped, dancing on their hind feet and lunging at the bars, all to so little avail that the painter hardly noticed. At last, at a word from their mistress, the dogs fell silent, or rather fell to whimpering and sniffing and running around in circles. The Princess, cautiously keeping well back lest Vlemk be some dangerous anarchist, leaned forward at the waist and, holding the leashes with one hand, shaded her eyes with the other, trying to make out whether she knew him. Suddenly she gave a start and cried, "Vlemk the box-painter!" Whether or not she had actually recognized him Vlemk could not tell. At very least, she had recognized his frock.

Vlemk sadly nodded. "Yes, Your Highness," he said, it's Vlemk."

"For heaven's sake, what are you doing here?" asked the Princess. "Surely you don't think we give handouts!"

"No," said Vlemk, "I have no reason to think that."

"What is it, then?" asked the Princess, a little more kindly.

For a long moment Vlemk said nothing, so sunk in misery that he could barely draw a breath. At last he pulled himself together and said: "I will tell you the truth, since then at least I will have it off my chest. It's not that I expect any good to come of it."

"Very well," said the Princess, and abruptly, as if at a premonition, dropped her gaze and went slightly pale.

"I have come," said Vlemk, "to ask for your hand in marriage." He was so embarrassed by the words, though he couldn't help saying them, that he wrung his hands and stared fixedly at the knobs of his shoes.

To her credit, the Princess did not laugh. "That is an exceedingly odd request," she said, and glanced up at him, then away. "As a man who's had dealings with wealthy aristocrats, you must surely be aware that it's unusual for members of the royal family to marry box-painters."

Even the dogs seemed to notice that something was taking place. They abruptly stopped their antics and stood motionless, their heads slightly tipped, like the heads of jurors.

"Yes," said Vlemk, "I'm aware of that."

"No doubt you're also aware," the Princess continued, her voice slightly husky, as if her heart were beating too fast, "that I saw you this morning in the gutter with some bottles and papers and the remains of a cat." Now she too tipped her head, studying him. Whether or not she was smiling Vlemk could not be sure in the enfolding darkness.

"Yes, I'm aware of that too," Vlemk said. The memory so abashed him that he was unable to say another word.

But as luck would have it, the Princess took over his argument for him. "I suppose you will say," she said, "that you are nevertheless an aristocrat, in your way, and worthy of any princess alive, since no one in the world is your equal at painting little boxes."

Poor wretched Vlemk could only nod and wring his hands and make his knuckles hurt. In the palace behind the Princess the windows were now all lighted—so many lighted windows it was like snow in the air. Above the highest tower, the moon was just breaking free of clouds.

"An interesting argument," the Princess said, though the argument was her own. She touched her forehead with the tips of three fingers and gave her head a queer, just perceptible jerk. "But I'm afraid I'm not persuaded. How can I know that, living as you do, you haven't lost all your former ability?"

At this, Vlemk's gift of speech rushed back. "Believe me," he said recklessly, "I could paint you a picture of your face so real it seems to speak!"

"Interesting," said the Princess thoughtfully. "Make it actually speak, and I'll permit you to talk with me again about these matters." So saying, giving him a mysterious smile—perhaps mocking, perhaps affectionate; in the frail moonlight and the glow of the palace not even a wizard could have decided for sure—she turned from him, gave a little tug at the leashes, and walked away toward the arched palace door with her greyhounds.

"Make it actually speak!" thought the artist, his heart beating wildly. It was hopeless, of course. Though a man had ten times the talent of poor Vlemk, no amount of care and skill could make a painting so true to its original that it could speak. If he couldn't make a painting so perfect that it could speak the Princess would never again talk to him. And if he couldn't find some way to talk further with the Princess—bask in that beauty that had struck him like an arrow in the chest this morning—how was he to paint? He was boxed in for certain, this time!

On the other hand, he thought, walking more rapidly down the hill toward the city, perhaps it *was* possible. It was, after all, an effect he'd never before attempted. The idea grew on him, and when he reached the city limits he was running full tilt, his long white artist's frock flying out behind him, his hat mashed down on his head under one long hand.

"Ah, he's himself again," said the regulars at the tavern as Vlemk ran by. The four—the barmaid and the three who carried arms—said nothing.

He ran full tilt, as if devils were chasing him, until he came to his house, paused only long enough to jerk open his door and slam it shut behind him, then ran full tilt up the stairs to his studio in the attic, overlooking the city. He sorted through his boxes, took the best he had on hand, and began on his project that same night.

2

WHEN VLEMK HAD WORKED for six weeks without sleeping, he began to get morbid, unsettling ideas. Sometimes it crossed his mind that what the Princess had said to him might be nothing but a grim, unfeeling joke, that she had no intention whatsoever of marrying him, indeed, that her purpose in giving him the seemingly impossible task was simply to make sure that he never again spoke to her. As an artist, he had difficulty believing such things, for if one gives in to the notion that visions of extraordinary beauty are mere illusion, one might as well cut off one's hands and sit on street-corners and beg. With all the strength of his carefully nourished and trained imagination, he cast back in his mind to that morning when he'd seen her in the carriage, peeking out through the curtains, and with all his dexterity and technical trickery he labored to set down that vision in paint. He could not doubt the intensity of the emotion that had surged in him or the accuracy of the vision he set down line by line. Every flicker of light in her pale blue eyes was precisely correct; the turn of the cheek, the tilt of the nose, the seven stray hairs on her forehead—all, insofar as they were finished, were indisputable.

Nevertheless, he was bedeviled by misgivings. It

occurred to him for instance that the paint was controlling him, creating not an image of the Princess but something new, a creature never before seen under the sun,
the painting growing like a plant under his brushes,
faithful to the form of its parent but unique, evolving
to singularity by sure, ancient laws—the white of the
earlobe calling to the white in the lady's eyes and demanding from the painter infinitesimal changes not
true to the actual lady but true, instead, to the natural
requirements of the picture on the box. It alarmed him
to discover that the throat was taking on, slowly but
inexorably, a greenish tint very rare if not unheard of
in human beings. "Yet why am I so fretful?" he rebuked
himself. "Is it not true that the emotion I feel when I
look at the painting is precisely the emotion I felt when
I looked at the lady, except for certain small mistakes
which can easily be fixed, such as the cock of the nostril
and the false glint of the eyelid?" He stood back and
looked at the painting to see if it was true. It was. "Then
all is still well," he said, moving the brush again, his
left eye closed, "let the throat be green as grass, so long
as it feels right!"

But that was the least of his misgivings. It struck him
that the feeling that had surged in him that morning was
mere chemistry, nothing more. "I'd drunk a good deal
the night before," he said aloud, bending over his table,
mixing paints. "Just as now if I straighten up suddenly,
tired as I am and tending toward dizziness, the room
will strike me differently than it would if I rose slowly,
so that morning—dehydrated, soaked to the bone with
dew and gutter wash—I must undoubtedly have seen
what I would not have seen at some other time, in some

other physiological condition. Is it possible that I'm painting not the Princess but, say, my own ureic acid level? my blood pressure?" The question vexed him, but even this misgiving he was able to quiet, to some extent, with the thought—which burst out of him when he was standing at the window looking down at the old crooked streets of the city—"Very well, my condition was abnormal that morning; but the abnormality was one very common among mortals—or anyway human beings—so that the vision can hardly be called freakish or divorced from reality." If the answer was not as comforting as the painter of boxes might have liked, it was nevertheless an answer, and Vlemk for a time went on painting.

But the greatest misgiving of all was this: the character of the face taking shape on the box was not altogether admirable. One saw faint but unmistakable hints of cruelty, vanity, and stinginess. He did his best, as any honest artist would have done, to undo them or overcome them, but the faults seemed ineradicable; they went, literally, to the bone. Vlemk stood patting his beard, pondering. It was not the first time he'd had this experience. Indeed, more often than not when he'd set out to capture some image which had given him pleasure, he'd found as he painted that the image, under scrutiny, proved slightly less appealing than he'd imagined. This had not much troubled him on those earlier occasions, because his purpose, then, had been simply to paint a pretty box. As a public minister unobtrusively rephrases the remarks of an irate king, fixing up the grammar, dropping out the swear words, here and there inserting a line or two that the people will perhaps find

more memorable, so Vlemk had offhandedly edited
Nature, straightening crooked stems, giving life to
drooping leaves, suppressing all traces of dog manure.
In the project at hand, that was, of course, impossible.
He began to perceive clearly the fact that he'd known
all along but had never quite confronted: that Beauty is
an artist's vain dream: it has, except in works of art,
no vitality, no body.

Abruptly, Vlemk found himself profoundly depressed. Slowly, meticulously, as if going through
empty emotions, he cleaned his brushes and carefully
capped his paints, saw to it that his oils and thinners
were exactly as they should be, removed his painter's
frock and hung it on its hook, then poked his arms into
his overcoat, stepped out of the studio, and locked the
door behind him.

At the tavern, things were just beginning to hum.
The regulars were singing and arguing politics; the
sullen, fat barmaid was pretending to smile in the arms
of an old drunken seaman. Old Tom was, as usual, asleep
under the stove.

"Ha!" cried one of the regulars as Vlemk came
through the door, "it's Vlemk the box-painter!"

Instantly, everyone smiled, delighted, for it was a
long time since they'd seen him. "Vlemk!" they shouted,
"where have you been? Pull up a chair!"

Soon poor Vlemk was as drunk as he'd ever been in
all his days, riding on a horse with a milk wagon behind
it—where he'd gotten the horse he had no idea—milk
bottles crashing on the cobblestone streets at every jolt
or sudden turn, bringing cats from every doorway; trees
careening by, looking drunker than he was; people on

the sidewalks going flat against the walls at his approach. Then, sometime later, he had no idea how long, though he dimly remembered sitting in some woman's apartment, staring with drunken fixity at the birthmark on her throat, he found himself chatting with some old, bony monk in a graveyard. They were sharing a bottle of some fennel-flavored drink.

"Ah yes," said the monk, "beauty is momentary in the mind, as the poet saith." He handed Vlemk the bottle. After a moment he continued, "I'll tell you how I got into this business in the first place. It had to do with women."

Vlemk tipped up the bottle and thoughtfully drank. The graves all around him tilted precariously then righted themselves.

"By the highest standards I am able to imagine, I have never known a beautiful woman," said the monk, "or even a good woman, or even a relatively good mother." He sighed and tapped the tips of his fingers together. "It occurred to me early on that since we can *conceive* of a beautiful woman, or a good woman, or even a relatively good mother, though we find none in Nature—always with the exception of Our Savior's Mother—" He cleared his throat as if embarrassed, and a quaver came into his voice as he continued, "It occurred to me early on that Nature is not worthy of our attention. Even the best we mortals can conceive, if we believe old books, is but a feeble reflection or aethereal vibration of the beauty God sits in the midst of, millenium to millenium."

Whatever more he had to say, Vlemk did not hear; he was fast asleep.

Sometime much later, as the sun was rising, Vlemk found himself standing at the door of his house, studying the doorway with tortuous attention, noting every stipple on the wall, every crack in the wood, making sure it was indeed his own doorway. He had never examined it quite so carefully before, which was perhaps the reason that, the more he looked, the more uncertain he was that the doorway was his own. What he did know, with certainty, was that the doorway was extremely interesting, as these things go. He ran his numb fingertips over the stone and cement and then, carefully, for fear of splinters, over the wood. He thought, for some reason, of the arched door of the palace where the Princess lived, and suddenly there welled up in him an emotion as curious as any he had ever experienced: pity for the Princess's doorway. It was not that there was anything wrong with that grand, solemn arch. Its proportions were perfect—though more appropriate, perhaps, for a church than for a palace. Its elegance was properly understated, its craftsmanship inspired though not original—the quatrefoils, the lozenges, the mournful beaked face that formed the keystone were all done to perfection. Yet the fact remained that, like his own humble doorway, it was obscurely ridiculous. No sooner had he thought this than he was ambushed by another thought more curious than the first. If he were to be granted, like St. John in the Bible, a vision of Heaven, he would certainly feel this exact same emotion, a faintly ironic amusement mixed with pity. Let all the architects of heaven and earth work together on the project, the result would be the same: not disappointing—nothing at all like that—but touchingly ridiculous.

Say heaven's gates were of pearl, and its streets pure gold. How could one look at those effects, however grand, without drawing back a little, with charitable amusement, thinking, "Ah, how labored! how dated!" One would recognize in a flash that the dragons on the pillars were Ming Dynasty, or Swedish, or French Imperial; that the structures were Mayan, or London 1840s, or Etruscan. Suppose to avoid this God made himself a heaven as humble as a shepherd's hut. "How artfully simple," one would say, as one said of a thousand such creations. Or suppose God chose in his infinite wisdom to make something brand new, unheard of on earth or on any other planet, matter or antimatter, black hole or white. "How new!" one would cry, and a billion billion other risen souls would cry the same, in antique harmony.

Thinking these thoughts, more pleasant than grim, for if they ruled out the ultimate value of all art, they gave mud beetles, humankind, and God a kind of oneness in futility, Vlemk opened the door and entered, hoping the house was indeed his house, still waiting for some sure sign. He found the stairway more or less where he'd expected he might find it, carefully avoided two sleeping cats, and began to climb. The bannister was as smooth as dusty, dry soap, like the bannister in his own house, which perhaps it was. When he came to the door to the studio, locked, he was virtually certain that this must be the place. He tried his key. It worked.

The first thing he saw when he entered the studio was his painting on the box, the Princess's face. With a start he realized that the picture was essentially finished. The lines he had doubted—the lines suggesting a touch of meanness in her character—were exactly right, no question about it, not that these were the most obvious of her lines. There was kindness too; generosity, a pleasing touch of whimsy. Indeed, an ordinary observer might never have noticed these slightly less pleasant qualities, though certainly they were there.

Vlemk sighed, pleased with the world in spite of its imperfections if not because of them—and made himself a large pot of coffee. The city below his window was still fast asleep except for, here and there, a garbage cart. He thought of the bony old monk in the graveyard, the woman with the birthmark. He poured himself coffee and sat looking at the painting on the box, smiling. Though she was a princess, she was no better, it seemed to him—though he knew that it might well be the alcohol—than the barmaid, the monk, the woman with the mark on her throat. Wherever the life-force could find a place to push it pushed, he mused—into barmaids, princesses, dandelions, monks, even box-painters. He laughed.

He was conscious of looking at the world as from a mountaintop. Yet even as he thought these serene, fond thoughts an uneasiness came over him. Make the picture speak, the Princess had said, *and I'll permit you to talk with me again about these matters.* It was true that she was beautiful, for all her faults, more beautiful than he'd ever before realized. If it was true that all the universe was one in its comic futility, it was also true that certain comically imperfect expressions of the universal force were for some reason preferable to others to any given life-expression, such as Vlemk. Having come to understand the Princess, both the best and the worst in her, poor Vlemk had fallen hopelessly, shamelessly in love. It was not some vague, airy vision now, it was something quite specific. He wanted to be in bed with her, talking, earnestly but in full detail, as if they had years to get everything right, about questions of Life and Art. He glanced down at his coffee. Did she perhaps prefer tea? He studied the painting. It told him nothing.

Abruptly, urgently, hardly knowing what he was doing, Vlemk uncapped his paints and seized a paint-brush. He painted furiously, with nothing in his mind, putting in without thought every beauty and deformity, working almost carelessly, almost wildly. Soon the painting was so much like the Princess that not even the Princess's mother could have told the two apart.

The picture began to speak. "Vlemk," it said, "I put a curse upon you: You shall never speak a word until I say so!"

Vlemk's eyes widened and he tried to protest, but already the curse was in effect; he was unable to make a sound.

3

NOW BEGAN A TERRIBLE PERIOD in the life of the box-painter. He had achieved what no artist before him had achieved, had succeeded in the most arduous love-task ever dreamt of, but the victory was ashes; he was as mute as a stone. If the picture remained stubborn, and Vlemk had no reason to doubt that it would, he would never in all his life say a word to the Princess, his love and inspiration.

He made feeble attempts at adjusting to his fate. Occasionally he'd take an order for a snuff-box with pansies on it, or a quill-box with a picture of the owner's house, but his work was inaccurate and shoddy; his heart had gone out of it. People began to haggle and try to put off paying him, even local doctors and bankers who could easily have afforded to pay if they'd wished to — a sure sign, as all box-painters know, that the work was no longer giving pleasure — and as the weeks passed business grew worse and worse; fewer and fewer people climbed the narrow stairs to his studio. That was just as well, in fact, for these days and nights Vlemk worked slowly or not at all. Even if he put in long hours, as he sometimes did in a fit of anxiety or anger turned inward, he got very little done. Ever since he'd finished his painting of the Princess, all other kinds of painting seemed beneath him, a betrayal of his gift. He found that he literally could not paint what was asked of him, and even if by dint of superhuman stubbornness he got through a given job, no one any longer praised his work, not even the stupidest oaf who came up off the street.

His fall was dramatically underscored, in Vlemk's mind, when occasionally, to his annoyance, some customer would glance unhappily from the painted box Vlemk had just finished for him to the box, nearby, on which he'd painted his portrait of the Princess. Sometimes they would say, "It looks real enough to speak!" "It does," the painting on the box would pipe up, and the customer would stare, disbelieving. Soon there were rumors that Vlemk had made a pact with the Devil. Business got still worse and eventually dropped away entirely.

"Woe is me," poor Vlemk would think, sitting alone in his studio, pulling at his knuckles. And if he didn't have troubles enough these days, the painting would start speaking again, complaining and criticizing, trying to offer helpful suggestions. "How can you call yourself a painter?" it would say in its ringing little voice, a voice not much louder than an insect's. "Where's your dedication? Is this what your disorderly habits have at last brought you down to?"

Vlemk would put up with this—or would leave for the tavern to get away from it—though it seemed to him brutally unfair, to say the least, that the masterpiece of his life should prove his curse and his soul's imprisonment. At times, throwing dignity to the winds, he would plead with his creation, imploring her in gesture—even going down on his knees to her—that she give him back his voice.

"No!" she would say.

"But why?" he would ask with his hands, fingers splayed wide and shaking.

"I don't feel like it," she said. "When I feel like it I will."

"You have no mercy!" he wailed in gesture, raising his fist and sadly shaking his head.

"*You* tell *me* about mercy!" cried the box. "You created me, you monster! Do you know what it's like, stuck here in one place like a miserable cripple, owning nothing in the world but a head and two shoulders — not even hands and feet?"

"Forgiveness is the greatest of all virtues," Vlemk would plead.

"No," the box would say. "The curse is still on!"

Vlemk would groan and say nothing more, would get up stiffly from his thick knees, and to punish the box in the only way he could, he would put on his hat and coat and descend to the street and make his way to the tavern.

Except for the inconvenience his poverty caused him, Vlemk could not honestly say he was sorry that his business as a box-painter had failed. It had never been a highly respected occupation, though people were amused by it. It had none of the prestige of gargoyle carving or stained-glass window making or the casting of bells, and to Vlemk, who believed himself vastly superior to those other, more respected artisans, it was a relief to become, for all practical purposes, a simple citizen, no longer an artisan looked down on by artisans he despised. His inability to speak, his inability even to whimper or grunt, soon made his anonymity complete.

He spent more and more of his time at the tavern, cadging the few coins he needed by holding out his hand and looking pitiful. His landlady was a problem, but only in the sense that it embarrassed him to meet her. The rumor of his friendship with the Devil kept her civil and distant.

It was winter now, picturesque in Vlemk's city if you were a rich man or only passing through. Icicles hung glittering from the eaves of every shop; snow put pointed hats on every housetop and steeple; horses in their traces breathed out hovering ghosts of steam. He was not altogether indifferent to all this. He observed with interest how shadows changed color behind a steam cloud, how the droplets on the nostrils of a horse gleamed amber in the sunlight. But his interest was tinged, inevitably, with gloom and anger. To Vlemk and those like him, cold weather meant misery and humiliation. His clothes were thin and full of holes to let in every wandering chill. "On *my* wages," thought Vlemk, bitterly joking—as was more and more his habit— "I'm lucky I can still afford skin." It was a joke worth saying aloud, he thought, but the curse prohibited it, so he stared straight ahead, living inside his mind, raising his glass with the others in the tavern, now and then joining in a fistfight if the cause seemed just.

Day after day, day after day, he would walk to the tavern as soon as it opened, trudging with great, gaping holes in his shoes over ice and through slush, hunched in his frayed old overcoat, snow piling up on his hat and shoulders, his fists clenched tight in his pockets that no longer held things. "What a box!" he would think, then would quickly shake his head as if the voice were someone else's, for he grew tired of his thoughts, now that he had no one to vent them on—tired and increasingly critical, for it had struck him, now that he must listen and not speak, that an incredible amount of what was said in the world was not worth saying.

As the cold settled in and the snow deepened, fewer and fewer strangers were to be found in the streets of Vlemk's city, and begging became increasingly difficult. Sometimes whole days went by when Vlemk couldn't gather enough coins for a single glass of wine. On these days Vlemk walked bent double from hunger pains— not surprisingly, since wine was now almost all he lived on. If he was lucky one of his unsavory friends—the petty thieves and marauders who gathered at the tavern every evening—would give him some of their wine; but the generosity of thieves is undependable. Sometimes their mood was wrong; sometimes they'd found nothing to burgle for weeks, so that their stomachs were as empty as Vlemk's.

"What am I to do?" his friend the ex-violinist would growl at him. "The rich have nothing but their money on their minds. They walk around the city with one hand on their billfold and the other on their pocketwatch." And with a stubborn, guilty look, he would drink his cheap wine, if he happened to have any, himself.

"Don't look at *me* with those mournful eyes," his friend the ex-poet would say to him. "Solomon in all his glory was not guarded and zipped like one of these!"

The axe-murderer—or rather would-be axe-murderer, for so far he'd never found the perfect occasion, the aesthetically perfect set of murder victims, and he was nothing if not a perfectionist—the axe-murderer would sit staring at the table with his icy stare, lost in thought—perhaps thoughts of killing Vlemk for his belt and shoelaces—and would let out not one word.

"I must do something," thought Vlemk. "Life is not fit to be endured if a man's cold sober!"

One night as this was happening—that is, as he was sitting at his table in the tavern with his misbegotten friends, clenching his belly against the hunger pains and shivering from the cold he had no wine to drive away— he saw the fat, sullen barmaid serve wine to a customer, a stooped old man with a white goatee, and leave his table without asking him to pay. In great agitation, Vlemk poked the poet with his elbow, pointed at the old man, and splashed his hands open to show he had a question. The poet studied him, managed the translation, then turned around to look at the old man.

"Oh, him," said the poet. "She always serves him free." He returned his attention to his drinking.

Again Vlemk poked him and splashed open his hands, this time raising his eyebrows as well and jerking his head forward, showing that his question was urgent.

" 'Why?' " said the poet, translating.

Eagerly, Vlemk nodded.

"The old man is a composer," said the poet. "Years ago he wrote the barmaid into an opera. She's showing her gratitude."

The axe-murderer slowly closed his eyes in disgust. So did the tomcat beside him. The ex-violinist looked depressed.

Abruptly Vlemk stood up, said good-bye with his hands, and hurried, bent over with hunger, to his freezing-cold studio. He painted all night like a man possessed, grimly ignoring the comments of the picture of the Princess, which stood watching, objecting in its piping, little voice to every stroke he set down. He painted quickly, easily, as he'd painted in the old days, perhaps because his project, however suspect, was his own idea and had a certain morbid interest. In the morning, when his new painted box-lid was finished, he went to curl up in his bed until the paint was dry. As soon as it was safe, he wrapped the painted box in a scrap of purple satin, which he'd stolen from the laundry chute weeks ago, and carried his gift through the slanting, soft snow to the barmaid.

When he set it on the bar, nodding and smiling, pointing from the box to the barmaid and back, the barmaid for a long time just stared at him. She had never really liked him — she liked almost no one, especially men, for she'd been badly used. Sometimes (Vlemk had noticed it only as he painted) she would come in bruised and battered from a night with some sailor who had strong opinions, or some farmer who knew only about cows. Sometimes — and this too he had remembered only when his brush reminded him — her eyes would suddenly fill with tears as she was pouring a glass of ale.

But at last the barmaid accepted the present, seeing that only if she did so would she ever be rid of him, and with a look oddly childlike, fearful and embarrassed, she removed the purple cloth. When the barmaid saw the painting she gave a cry like a brief yelp of sorrow and her lips began to tremble; but before you could count ten, the tremble became a smile, and she reached out with both plump hands for Vlemk's bearded face, drew it close, and kissed it.

Vlemk was bitterly ashamed, for nothing was ever less deserved than that kiss, but he forced himself to smile, and he smiled on, grimly, as the barmaid ran from table to table with her gift, showing it to the regulars one after another, all of whom heartily praised it.

No one seemed to know except the ex-poet, the ex-violinist, and the axe-murderer that the painting on the box was a lie, a fraud, an outrage. He'd given the barmaid a childlike smile, though it was as foreign to her sullen, lumpy face as Egypt to an Eskimo. He'd given her the eyes of a twelve-year-old milkmaid, though her own eyes had nothing but the exact same brown of the irises in common. He'd reddened her chin and removed certain blemishes, turning others — for example the birthmark on her throat, which he paid close attention to only as he painted it — to beauty marks. He'd lifted her breasts a little, tightened her skin, raised a sagging eyebrow, increased the visibility of her dimple. In short, he'd made her beautiful, and he'd done it all so cunningly that no one but an artist could have told you where the truth left off and the falsehood began.

"Wine for the box-painter!" cried one of the regulars.

"Wine whenever he wants it!" cried the barmaid, and abruptly, as if changed into some other person, she smiled.

The troubles of Vlemk the box-painter were over — or at any rate Vlemk's most immediate trouble. From that night on when he went to the tavern he got all he asked for, wine, beer, and whiskey until only with the help of a friend could he find his way home, and sometimes not even then. As for the barmaid, a curious thing happened. She became increasingly similar to the fraudulent painting, smiling as she served her customers, looking at strangers with the eyes of an innocent, standing so erect, in her foolish pride, that her breasts were almost exactly where Vlemk had painted them. The success of her after-hours business increased, so much so that Vlemk began to worry that perhaps she would get married and leave the bar, which would throw him back on begging. Sometimes to his distress, he would catch her stealing a little look at the box, which she kept prominently displayed, and once—far worse for Vlemk's sense of honor—she gave him a look that made him think for an instant that she *knew* what he had done. Why not, of course. Wasn't she also a dabbler in visions, a creator and destroyer? She said nothing, however; for which Vlemk was profoundly grateful.

With other people, Vlemk was all too often less fortunate. Because he was a mute now, people began telling him things, all of them eager to share their troublesome and shameful secrets, yet concerned that their secrets remain unknown. Women, looking into his gray, all-seeing eyes, and assured that he was voiceless, as safe as a boulder, would reveal to him such horrors of frustration and betrayal, remorse, inexpressable indignation, and despair, that his sleep would be troubled for weeks by alarming dreams. Gentle old men told him stories of rape and arson, cruelty to animals, and heaven knows what else. Vlemk the box-painter became a walking encyclopedia of the sins and transgressions of humanity—more scapegoat than priest, alas, since he was powerless to forgive or condemn.

He learned, among other things, why the poet no longer wrote poetry and the ex-violinist had turned in disgust against music.

"My audience," said the poet, lips trembling, eyebrows twitching, "has, collectively, the brains of one pig." He pursed his lips. "Perhaps that's unfair," he said. "Perhaps I underestimate pigs." This the poet said in Vlemk's studio, where no one could hear him but Vlemk and the painting of the Princess on the box, who said nothing. "What good is it," the poet asked, pacing up and down, flaxen hair flying, "telling my audience things they can never understand?" He puffed at his pipe, sending up angry little clouds, and continued, jabbing with his pipestem and pacing again, "*We* know, you and I, the sad truth of the matter: To fools, nothing *can* be said; to the wise, nothing *need* be said. Take all the wisdom of Homer and Virgil. We knew it in our hearts when we were four, you and I. — No, I'm serious, my friend!" He raised his hand as if Vlemk might find his voice and object. "Who learns anything — I say, *anything* — from poetry? Say I describe all the agony of love with magnificent precision, showing true and false, revealing the applications for the priesthood and men engaged in business. If I'm right, exactly and precisely right, what do you say — you, the reader? 'That's right,' you say, if you're wise and not a fool. What have I taught you, then? Nothing, of course! Nothing whatsoever! I have said, with a certain elegance, exactly what you know. And what does the fool say? Why, nothing, of course. 'I never really cared much for poetry,' says he. 'I like a man to say what he means.' Poetry's a trinket, then, a luxury and amusement, a kind of secret handshake between equals. Nothing wrong with that, of course. It's an occupation no worse than, say, being a cook" — his lips twisted to a sneer — "a cook, ha ha!, a man whose art is consumed and goes sliding back to earth!" He heaved a deep sigh. "I have therefore abandoned that paltry mistress poesy." He stood now angrily gazing down at the crooked little streets. "I have put my intelligence to more interesting uses," he said quietly, glancing past his shoulder. "I steal people's jewelry. I kidnap people's children. That surprises you?"

Vlemk shrugged.

"I do not kill people," said the poet, "that's against my principles! I merely upset them a little — teach them values, like Goethe and Schiller."

Vlemk nodded. It crossed his mind that if his friend the ex-poet was really a jewel-thief and kidnaper of children he'd be a good deal better off than he was; but Vlemk let it go. Poetic license. It was true — Vlemk knew because he'd seen it — that the man picked pockets and stole eggs.

The violinist said, not many nights later, sitting in the abandoned railroad car which was his temporary home, "I have only one real ambition in life: getting even."

Vlemk splashed his hands open and lifted his eyebrows.

" 'Who?' you say," said the ex-violinist, translating. His spectacles flashed, catching a little light from the candle on the crate between them. "Audiences, composers, conductors, violin makers. . . . Everyone's my enemy! Why should I make exceptions?" He passed Vlemk the crackers and chianti, for in small things he was generous, and the chianti had turned. The ex-violinist sat grinding his teeth, his fingertips trembling, then continued very softly, "You have to understand how it is for us performers. Some fool writes a piece and we interpret with all our hearts, but there's nothing to interpret, just the noises a fool makes, or if there's something there the conductor gets the tempo wrong, or the audience dislikes it because they've heard on good authority that all Slavs are sentimental. At best, a string on the violin breaks." Loudly, he cracked his knuckles, all ten of them in rapid succession, so that a shudder ran down Vlemk's back. Though the light in the railroad car was dim — too dim for Vlemk to make out what the creatures were, moving now and then in the corners — it seemed to Vlemk that as he spoke there were tears in the ex-musician's eyes. "Thousands of dollars worth of music lessons, thousands of arpeggios and scales — for that! Very well!" He sucked in breath. "There are other uses for dexterity like mine!"

Vlemk raised his eyebrows and opened his hands.

The musician leaned forward, confidential, trembling violently. "I steal valuables from purses in coatrooms," he said. "There's no real money in it, but the response of the crowd is tremendous."

Vlemk had long made a point of never being alone with the third of his unsavory friends, the axe-murderer, but one night in January, when he ducked into a doorway to avoid an icy rain, that too happened. The axe-murderer was a sombre man with thick, hairy forearms, short, thick legs, and a neck as big around as a large man's thigh. He had a mouth made unpleasant by small, open sores, and eyes that seemed never to focus on anything but to stare with malevolent discontent in whatever direction his small, shiny head was turned. He rarely spoke, but tonight, pinned shoulder to shoulder beside Vlemk in the doorway, waiting for the rain to stop—the street full of shadows, the lamps not yet lit— the murderer abruptly, for no reason, broke his rule. "Vlemk," he said, in a voice as low and gravelly as a frog's, "the trouble with you is, you're insensitive to the power of evil."

Vlemk nodded, shuddering, and made an effort to look thoughtful. He craned his head forward, thinking the rain was perhaps lighter than he'd imagined, but the shoulder of the murderer pinned him tightly against the doorjamb, and he soon realized that the pressure against him was intentional; he was meant to stay, hear the murderer out, listen attentively, as if his life depended on it, for indeed, conceivably, it did.

"You have a strange point of view," said the axe- murderer. "It seems to you quite normal, because the herd of humanity generally shares it; but believe me your view is in fact both strange and irrational."

Again Vlemk nodded.

"You look for Beauty in the world," said the axe- murderer. "You formulate impressions in the archaic vocabulary of Grace. This is a mistake. What the intelli- gent man looks for is *interest*. Look at our friends the ex-poet and the ex-musician. They started out as pur- suers of Beauty, devotees of supernatural premises. What are they now?" He laughed so deep in his throat it might have come from a well. "They are retired, my friend. And even in retirement they have no more under- standing of the truth than a pair of fat ducks." He turned his sore-specked, expressionless face, allowing the eyes to bore coldly into Vlemk. "I, on the other hand," he said, "am not retired. Actually, strictly speaking, I haven't yet begun. Many people say I will never begin, but I spit in their eyes." He glanced downward, indicating that Vlemk should do the same, and from under the skirt of his overcoat showed the blade of an axe.

Vlemk swallowed and quickly nodded. The rain was beginning to let up now, but still the firm pressure of the murderer's shoulder boxed him in.

"You're an idealist, Vlemk," said the axe-murderer. "Reality, you think, is what might be, or what peeks from behind what is. What evidence have you for this shadow you prefer to the hard, smelly world we exist in? Look again!" Again they looked down, both of them, at the axe. "Reality is matter in all its magnificent complexity," said the murderer, "the sludge of actuality in infinite mechanical aspiration. Break the machine and you begin to know its usefulness! Close off the view of the mountains with a curtain and you begin to see the glory of the view." He pressed harder against Vlemk and asked with a sneer, "You imagine you search out Reality, painter of little boxes?" He laughed. "You're an evader and avoider! I give you my assurance — experience is the test — chop off the heads of a family of seven, let the walls and the floors be splashed with their blood, let the dogs howl, the cats flee, the parakeets fly crazily in their filthy wicker cages, then ask yourself: *is* this or *is this not* Reality? — this carnage, this disruption of splendid promise? Take the blinders from your eyes! Death and Evil are the principles that define our achievements and in due time swallow them. Ugliness is our condition and the basis of our interest. Is it our business to set down lies, or are we here to tell the Truth, though the Truth may be unspeakably dreadful?"

Vlemk nodded slowly and thoughtfully and pursed his lips.

The murderer's face grew more sullen than usual, and when he spoke again his grumble was so low and disheartened that Vlemk could barely hear him. "Admittedly all this is as yet still a little theoretical. The police are everywhere, and how is one to get proper coverage? The newspapers suppress things, edit things. I'm like you, my friend Vlemk, if what I hear about the picture of the Princess is true: a genius who's never reached his audience." He chuckled, miserable as a snake. Suddenly the murderer drew in one sharp breath and became still all over, his hand clamped firm as a vise on the box-painter's arm. "Perhaps this is it!" he whispered. A family of five was entering the old empty church across the street, ducking in out of the rain, perhaps. As soon as the door closed behind them, the murderer stepped softly from the doorway, tipping up his coat-collar and pulling down his hat, then hurried away through the rain to the farther curb. At once, before the murderer could change his mind, Vlemk set off, almost running, in the direction of the tavern. He need not have hurried. When he met the axe-murderer the following night he learned that, as usual, he'd done nothing. Nothing, as usual, had been quite as he required. For some arts, the difficulties are all but insurmountable.

4

So Vlemk's life continued, day after day and week after week. Insofar as possible, he kept himself drunk. In due time, were it not for the picture, he might have forgotten his unhappiness and learned to be content.

But the talking picture of the Princess would give him no rest. It complained and nagged until he was ready to throw it out the window; yet complaint and unpleasantness were by no means all that the picture was capable of. Sometimes when Vlemk was so sunk in gloom that it took him all his strength to raise his chin from his fists and his elbows from his knees, the picture would speak to him so kindly, with such gentle understanding, that he would burst into tears. At such moments it grieved him that he'd abandoned his profession, that all order had gone out of his life, all trace of dignity. He wrung his hands and ground his teeth and looked longingly at the brushes laid in shabby disarray on the table.

"Well, why don't you paint, then?" said the picture on the box, who had been watching him narrowly for some time. "It can make you no more miserable than you are!"

"Ha!" Vlemk thought, "you know nothing!" He wished with all his heart that he could say it aloud, but owing to the curse he could speak not a single syllable,

37

even to the box. "*No* one knows anything!" he wanted
to say, for the opinions of his friends had persuaded him.
"We artists are the loneliest, most miserable people in
the world, misunderstood, underestimated, scorned and
mocked, driven to self-betrayal and dishonesty and star-
vation! We're masters of skills more subtle than the
skills of a wizard or king, yet we're valued less highly
than the moron who carves out stone statues with no
reference to anything, or sticks little pieces of colored
glass together, or makes great brass bell-molds in endless array, the first one no different from the last one!"

"Does it help," asked the picture, "to stand there
shaking your fists like that?"

Vlemk the box-painter whirled around, furious, intending to shout obscenities at the picture on the box,
though of course he could shout nothing. His face became red as a brick and his eyes bulged, and his breathing was so violent that it seemed he would surely have
a heart attack. But at once he changed his mind and put
his hands over his face, for he'd seen again, staring at the
picture, that the Princess was too beautiful for words.

"What is it?" asked the picture. "What is it that so
upsets you?" She spoke with great kindness and what
seemed to Vlemk sincere concern, so that he could only
assume that she'd forgotten that she'd put the curse on
him. (In this he was mistaken.) He tried mouthing words
at her, but the picture only stared at him as if in puzzle-
ment, and at last Vlemk gave up in despair and turned
sadly away. Tears began to brim up in his eyes and drip
down his cheeks.

"It's nothing strange," thought Vlemk, clenching and
unclenching his fists. "She fills me with sorrow for what

I might have had but lost, this vision of extraordinary beauty I've painted on the box." He ground his teeth and wiped away the tears, but at once his eyes were filled again. "Vision," he thought woefully, and began to shake his head like a child. "Vision, yes, nothing but a vision — a romantic illusion!" Suddenly he bent over, sobbing.

"Poor Vlemk!" cried the box in its piping little voice. "Oh poor, poor Vlemk!" If he'd turned around to look, he might have seen to his astonishment that the box was crying too. But he did not turn. He sobbed for a long time, deaf to the peeping sobs behind him; then at last, with a great, broad shudder and a grinding of his teeth, he got hold of himself. What a fool he was being! There was no way on earth she could have forgotten that it was she who'd put the curse on him. She was a charmer, his pretty little picture, but mean as a snake! And if the picture had no heart, what of the Princess?

"I've been a dolt," he thought. "The murderer's quite right. I must rid myself of idiotic visions!"

With eyes like a maniac's he went over to the hook where his artist's frock hung, carefully took it down, and poked his arms in. He went back to the table where his brushes lay, uncapped a bottle of thinner, poured just a little into a dish, unbuttoned and rolled up his sleeves, then, more meticulous than a surgeon over his knives, began the exceedingly delicate business of cleaning and trimming his brushes. Then he squeezed paint onto his palette and poured oil and glaze into their containers. When all this was ready, he chose a box — a beautiful one of rosewood — and began to paint.

The picture of the Princess watched with interest.

"Another picture of me?" she asked after a time.

"Every painter," thought Vlemk, in lieu of giving answer, "has his own proper subject. Some are best at cliffs, some at trees and flowers, some at boats, some at cows crossing a stream, some at churches, some at babies. *My* proper subject—the subject which for some reason engages me heart and soul—is the Princess's face."

For several hours, Vlemk painted with such intensity that it seemed he might explode.

Suddenly the picture said, "*I* don't look like that!"

Vlemk turned, nodded with a mysterious dark smile at the picture on the box, then coolly turned away again, back to his work.

He was painting as he'd never before painted in his life, gazing, unflinching, into the abyss. Every hint his memory of her face provided him, or his increasingly sure knowledge of her perfect twin, the picture he'd earlier painted on the box—the face now watching him in dismay and indignation—he pursued relentlessly, as a surgeon edges into a cortex, following a cancer with the tip of his knife. He softened nothing, gave in nowhere, but set down the Princess's flaws in bold relief. Nothing escaped him: the fullness of the lower lip which only now, as it helplessly submitted to his brush, did he recognize for what it was, a latent sensualism that, if pushed as he pushed it now in paint, fulfilling its dark potential, might be the Princess's ruin; the infinitesimal weakness of one eyelid, its barely perceptible inclination to droop; the even less perceptible but nevertheless real inclination toward hairiness on her upper lip and chin, should her diet fall into disorder, her hormones lose balance. It was a terrible experience, painful and alarming, yet at the same time morbidly thrilling. Both about seeing and about finding new ways to give expression to what he saw, he was discovering more in a single night, it seemed to him, than he'd discovered up to now in all his life.

"That's stupid," said the picture on the box behind him, crossly. "You've missed the likeness. I'm not like that at all!"

"Well, you know, it's just *Art*," Vlemk answered inside his mind, ironically joking, playing fool in the ancient way of angry artists. Deny it as she might, he thought—and heaven knew she was stupid enough; it was visible in the eyes—she would perhaps not miss it entirely, but feel, at some animal level, rebuked. Behind and to the left of the lady he was painting, he fashioned a small monkey at a pulpit, reading a Bible and shaking his finger, a blazing arched window behind him, obscuring his outlines. Her case, the image was meant to say, was not quite hopeless. If she turned, she might yet receive instruction, if only from a monkey.

The painting that could speak was saying nothing. She had closed her eyes and put on, to punish him, a bored look, or worse than bored: a bored person frozen alive. He felt a brief flash of anger and impatience, then suddenly a kind of joy, though dark and subterranean: she'd given him inspiration for another painting. This time, he decided, he would work more purely, in absolute isolation, that is, outside the influence of her judging eyes. Carefully, as if fondly, he lifted the box with the painting that could speak and carried it to the darkest corner of his studio, where he set it down on a chair and covered it with a cloth.

"What are you dong?" the picture protested. "Take me back where I was! I don't like it here!"

Vlemk, of course, said nothing but returned to his paints.

It was morning now. Light was streaming in, and chickens and dogs in the city below were calling from street to street like peddlers, their voices bouncing over the ice. Vlemk made coffee, thought briefly of getting a little rest, then settled down on his stool, at his slanted table—methodically, neatly, with controlled but white hot concentration—to begin on his new work, "The Princess Looking Bored." The lines seemed almost to fall from his brush, the idea taking shape with the naturalness and ease of a flower's opening—though a terrible flower, needless to say: a bloom almost certainly poisonous. As with the painting he'd worked on through the night, he pursued the Princess's worst potential with the reckless abandon of a lover in a fury, a husband betrayed. It was an eye-opener. Who would have guessed (who did not know her as Vlemk knew her) what depths of deceit and self-deception she was capable of, how pitiful and self-destructive her stratagem, or the measure of panic and self-doubt behind the mask of disdain? No wonder she held out on him, refused to lift the curse! He could understand now the dream of the axe-murderer, standing in the midst of his butchery, and he at the same moment recognized with immense satisfaction, that his art was as much above that of the murderer as was the murderer's above that of the man who carved bestial fantasies in pious stone. Vlemk painted quickly, fanatically, yet precisely, like a virtuoso violinist scattering notes like leaves in a wind. Not that he worked, like his friend the ex-violinist, to get even. Nothing could have been farther from the box-painter's mind. His work was absolutely pure; it had no object but knowledge—and Ah! thought Vlemk, what knowledge he was getting! "Princess, how well I know you," he said inside his mind, "you have no idea!" From the chair in the corner came occasional peeps of distress. He ignored them.

He painted all day, finished the second of his Reality boxes, as he jokingly called them, rested for an hour, then went down—his head full of new ideas—to the tavern. As in the days of his innocence (so he thought of them now), his unwinding was like a frenzy. Though he'd meant to remain fairly sober and eat some food, since his heart was full of plans and he was eager to get back to his studio, he'd forgotten his intentions by the second drink. He was painting, after all, as no other box-painter in the world could paint, making discoveries as rare as any scientist's. He was coming to such a grasp of life's darkest principles—and at the same time discovering, as he chased his intuitions, such a wealth of technical tricks and devices—that not a dozen fat books could contain what he had learned in one day. He was achieving, in a word, such mastery of his art, and he was filled with such pleasure in what fortune had granted him, that he could not possibly sit quietly for just one drink, then quietly trudge home. He held the barmaid on his lap and patted her knee, made scornful faces at the poet, whose poverty of wit he despised, mocked the ex-musician by pretending, voicelessly, to sing to him, even once recklessly shook his fist at the axe-murderer. He awakened the following morning in a cellar—

he had no idea of how he'd gotten there—his trousers
smelling powerfully of duck manure, as if he'd walked
through some pond, his head pounding fiercely, his
hands so shaky it would be hours, he knew, before he
could steady his fingers sufficiently to pick up a paint-
brush. Swearing at himself inside his mind, he got up,
found his bearings—for he'd wandered to the squalid
lower rim of the city—and went home.

"So you've decided to leave me here hidden under
a cloth for the rest of my natural days? Is that your
intention?" called the picture that could talk.

Grudgingly Vlemk went over and lifted the cloth
away.

"Good heavens!" cried the picture, eyes wide. "Are
you all right?"

Vlemk scowled, pulled at his beard, and went to bed.

Again that night he painted until dawn, made coffee,
then worked on yet another box all through the day.
Each box was more sinister than the last, more shamelessly debauched, more outrageously unfair in the opinion of the picture that could talk, which she now did
rarely, too angry and too deeply hurt to give Vlemk the
time of day. When his work was finished he again went
to the tavern, where he again got so drunk he had no
memory of what happened and staggered home as the
milkmen were beginning their rounds.

For several weeks this frenzy of painting and drinking continued, and then one day in March—standing
in his roomful of boxes with pictures of the Princess
on them, each picture meaner and uglier than the last,
some so deformed by the painter's rage to tell the truth
unvarnished that you could make out no face—Vlemk

abruptly stopped. Why he stopped he could hardly have
said himself. Partly it was this: whether or not it was
true that his work was magnificent, as he sometimes
imagined, no one came to see it, and when he carried
a box with him to the tavern, no one liked it, not even
the axe-murderer.

"How can you not like it?" Vlemk asked angrily with
his hands.

"Borrrring," said the axe-murderer, and turned his
head away, staring through the wall.

"Ha," thought Vlemk, hardly hiding his scorn, "*your*
work is interesting, *my* work is boring."

But Vlemk, being no fool, understood the implications. It was exactly as the half-wit ex-poet had said:
we learn nothing from art, merely recognize it as true
when it happens to be true; no law requires that we be
thrilled by it. Not that he would have said Science is
any better. "What are the grandest proofs of Science,"
Vlemk thought, "but amusements, baubles, devices for
passing time, like the game of quoits? 'Science,' you may
say, 'improves life, even when it makes it longer.' Yes,
that's true. Let us be grateful to scientists, then, for their
valuable gifts to us, as we are grateful to cows for milk,
or pigs for bacon. As the brain's two lobes work dissimilar problems, Science and Art in dissimilar ways
try to work out the truth of the universe. This activity
the Scientist or Artist finds comforting to his ego, and
it provides him with Truths he can make gifts to the
world as a gentleman gives his lady a locket. And what
if the truth about the universe is that it's boring?"

So Vlemk gradually came to the conclusion that his
joy in his work, like his earlier vision of extraordinary

beauty, was delusion. It was not that he denied having
enjoyed himself, learning the techniques by which he
nailed down his, so to speak, vision—his perception,
that is, of the fragility and ultimate rottenness of things.
So one might enjoy learning the technique of the mandolin, but when one finished one was only a mandolin
player. One might as well have studied the better and
worse ways of sitting on a porch.

So Vlemk, with bitter little jokes to himself, stopped
painting. The talking picture sulked as much as ever,
and from time to time it crossed Vlemk's mind that perhaps if he looked he could find some tourist who might
buy it off him; but for one reason or another, he did not
sell it. He settled down now to a life of serious, uninter-
rupted dissolution, never washing his face or changing
his clothes, never for a moment so sober that he remembered to feel regret. Days passed, and weeks, and Vlemk
became so changed that, for lack of heart, he gave up
all his former rowdiness, and often not even regulars
at the tavern seemed to know him as he groped his way
past them, bent and glum as the Devil in his chains, on
his way to the bathroom or to the alley. He forgot about
the Princess, or remembered her only as one remembers
certain moments from one's childhood. Sometimes if
someone spoke of her—and if it was early in the evening, when Vlemk was still relatively sober—Vlemk
would smile like a man who knows more than he's telling about something, and it would cross people's minds,
especially the barmaid's, that Vlemk and the Princess
were closer than one might think. But since he was a
mute and declined to write notes, no one pressed him.
Anyway, no one wanted to get close to him; he smelled
like an old sick bear.

Things went from bad to worse for Vlemk the box-painter. He no longer spoke of life as "boxing him in," not only because the expression bored him but also, and mainly, because the box had become such an intransigent given of his existence that he no longer noticed.

Then one May morning as he was lying in a gutter, squinting up bleary-eyed and exploring a newly broken tooth with his tongue, a carriage of black leather with golden studs drew up beside him and, at a command from the person inside, came to a stop.

"Driver," said a voice that seemed as near as Vlemk's heart, "who is that unfortunate creature in the gutter?"

Vlemk turned his head and tried to focus his eyes, but it was useless. The carriage was like a shadow in a fire too bright to look at, a gleam of sunlight on a brilliantly glazed, painted box-lid.

"I'm sorry, Princess," said the driver, "I have no idea."

When he heard it was the Princess, Vlemk thought briefly of raising one hand to hide his face, but his will remained inactive as he lay as he was.

"Throw the poor creature a coin," said the Princess. And let us hope he's not past using it."

After a moment something landed, plop, on Vlemk's belly, and the carriage drove away. Slowly, Vlemk moved one hand toward the cool place—his shirt had lost its buttons, and the coin lay flat on his pale, grimy skin where at last his groping fingers found it and dragged it back down to the ground where it would be safe while he napped. Hours later he sat up abruptly and realized what had happened. He looked down at his hand. There lay the coin, real silver with a picture of the King on it.

"How strange!" thought Vlemk.

When he'd gotten to his feet and moved carefully to the street-corner, touching the walls of the buildings with the knuckles of one cupped hand, he found that he had no idea where he was, much less how he'd gotten there, and no idea which direction to take to reach his house. When he waved to hurrying passers-by, looking at them helplessly and silently moving his loose, mute mouth, they ducked their heads, touching their hats, and hurried around him as they would if he were Death. He edged on alone, hunting for some landmark, but it was as if all the streets of the city had been moved to new locations. He shook his head, still moving his mouth like some mechanical thing, not a living man, wholly unaware that he was doing it. An old sick alley-cat opened his mouth in a yawn, showing teeth like needles, then closed it again and lowered his head. In his right hand Vlemk clenched—so tightly that the rim of it bit into his flesh—the coin with the picture of the King on it.

5

THREE DAYS LATER, having carefully considered from every point of view, having bathed away the filth and trimmed his beard and washed his old black suit in the sink in the studio, and having dried it on the railing of the balcony, Vlemk the box-painter started across the city and up the hill toward the Royal Palace. Tucked under his arm, he carried the box with the talking picture. In his pocket he had a carefully folded note which he'd meticulously lettered, intending to put it in her hand as he gave her the box. *"Dear Princess,"* the note read, *"Here is the gift I said I would try to make for you, a picture so real it can speak. I release you from your promise to talk with me, since misfortune has made me a mute, perhaps for my impertinence. I hope this finds you well. Respectfully, Vlemk the Box-Painter."*

He arrived at the palace, as he had planned to do, just at the time when the Princess would be coming in from walking her dogs. The last of the sunset was fading from the clouds, exactly as last time; the moon was bright; here and there pockets of fog were taking shape, intruding on the smoothly mown slopes from ponds and woods. He approached exactly as he'd approached before, but to Vlemk's dismay, first one thing was different and then another, so that in the end the palace seemed

49

changed entirely. The outer gates of iron had been thrown wide open and there were no guards in sight, so that he wondered for a moment if the greyhounds, when they saw him, would not tear him to bits; but all around the front of the palace stood carriages and large outdoor lanterns, dozens and dozens of them, flickering merrily, as if vying with the stars, and near the arched front door he had once felt pity toward, aristocrats stood talking and laughing, drinking champagne in their splendid dress. It was unlikely, he thought, that they would stand there and watch the dogs kill him — though on the other hand Vlemk had learned enough from people's secrets, to be aware that in these matters nothing is ever quite certain.

But the dogs, he thought the next instant, were the least of it. How could he walk in, in the middle of a party of lords and ladies, and give the Princess his present? How would he even find her? As he drew nearer, moving slowly now, he saw that the lords and ladies' clothes were all of the finest material, with clasps and buckles, buttons, epaulettes, and swordhilts of gold and silver. He looked down at his knobby brown shoes, white worksocks, and baggy black trousers, then at his vest, riding like a saddle on his pot-belly. It had only three buttons — two gray ones and a blue one. His coat had no buttons at all. He stood staring, with the box clamped tightly under his elbow, thinking what a fool he'd been, seeing himself as the Princess and her highborn friends would see him: gray-streaked unmanageable hair to his shoulders, a number of veins in his face broken, the slope of his shoulders and the bend of his back the realized potential of a life of disorder and dissolution. "I had better go back home," he thought. "I'll catch her sometime when she's not busy."

From under the black velvet cloth the picture called, "What's the matter? Why are we stopping?"

Vlemk brought the box out from under his arm, held it in front of him, and like a waiter unfolding a napkin with the back of his hand, tipped off one corner of the cloth so that the picture could see.

For a moment the face on the box only stared, abashed. At last, in a piping voice smaller than usual the picture said, "The Princess must be having a party."

If he'd been hoping the picture would resolve his dilemma, Vlemk was disappointed. He should hardly have been surprised. She might look like the Princess, might have the very same intelligence and emotional make-up, but all that those painted blue eyes had ever seen before this walk was the box-painter's studio.

"What shall we do?" she asked.

As Vlemk stood irresolute, the answer was thrust upon them. The ground began to tremble and a sound like distant thunder began to rise from behind a dark clump of trees. A moment later six or seven horses came bounding over a hill into the light of the lanterns, on their backs young highborn men and women in capes and riding hats, returning, with the greyhounds at their heels, from a gallop over the grounds. Not far from where the others stood drinking their champagne, the riders reined in and the horses came trotting up, docile as sheepdogs; then, before the first of the horses had stopped, the greyhounds saw Vlemk and, barking like devils, came shooting out, bounding like deer, toward him. Instantly the horsemen wheeled after them, hurrying to the rescue—or so Vlemk prayed.

The greyhounds came flashing through the darkness like knives, with astonishing speed and clarity of purpose, but the horsemen were close behind, shouting stern orders at the dogs and hurried good advice to Vlemk, if only he could have heard what they were shouting. It was a horseman who reached him first; the dogs held back at the last minute. The rider was a tall young man with a moustache, his cape like midnight except for the gleaming pure white of the lining, thrown back jauntily past his shoulder like a wing. He shouted something which Vlemk could not make out, then shouted it again. Now the others came swerving and slanting up around him—one of them, he saw, was the Princess. He was suddenly conscious of the late-June warmth and wetness in the air. She did not look at all as she'd looked before, but even with his heart pounding wildly in his throat from the scare they'd given him, Vlemk knew at once what the changes were—the make-up, the hair, the padded square shoulders, the startling spring paleness of skin and the hollowness of her cheeks. Fasting? he wondered. He tried to recall if some religious holiday was at hand. Two of her friends were on the ground now, quieting the dogs. The tall young man with the moustache bent down from the saddle. "Who are you?" he shouted to Vlemk. "What are you doing here?"

Vlemk threw a look at the Princess for help, but she kept back, remote and cautious, almost ghostly. Her horse pranced and turned, eager to be gone, and from time to time the Princess glanced back at the people who'd been drinking by the door, now all hurrying in a crowd to find out what was happening. Seeing that there was no other way, Vlemk reached into his pocket and drew out the card, unfolded it with badly shaking fingers, and handed it to the man. The man came close, apparently having difficulty reading it in the moonlight. He half smiled, then wheeled around and trotted his horse to the Princess. "It's for you," he said.

The Princess did not reach for it. "What does it say?"

"You think I read your mail?" he said, smiling like a lover, and held it nearer, insisting that she take it. Vlemk glanced down, full of gloom and a curious detachment, as if the Princess were an acquaintance from some other life and they had both changed completely. His gaze happened to fall on the box. She was watching the Princess and the man in the moustache with sharp, almost furious disapproval.

The Princess did take the note at last, giving the man a little smile, half cross, half playful. When she had finished reading she glanced sharply at Vlemk. "You are Vlemk the box-painter?" she asked, displeased. He nodded. She seemed to make out, now, the box under his arm. She looked around — the people with the champagne glasses were drawing near — and at last she said, "Bring him where it's light," and, without another glance, assuming their obedience, she set off at a trot toward the lanterns. "I don't like her," said the picture on the box, emphatically. Vlemk covered the tiny painted mouth with his hand. Now the moustached man was bending down again, reaching to offer Vlemk a lift up and ride. Vlemk stared a moment before he saw what was intended, then shook his head in alarm and hurried on foot after the Princess. When she reached the lanterns she stopped again for a moment and looked back at him, then nodded, as if telling him to follow, and rode straight on to the enormous, arched front door. There she dismounted, gave the reins to a servant, and stood waiting for Vlemk to catch up with her. As soon as he did, panting from exertion and hastily covering the face with the cloth, the Princess said, "Won't you come inside?" Without waiting for an answer she started up the wide marble stairs.

Vlemk was by this time well aware that by bringing the box to the Princess he had made a mistake. There were social implications he hadn't bothered to think through, implications that now, too late, he recognized as painful to the Princess. Either she must curtly and crudely dismiss him, a poor harmless mute—which was not in her nature—or she must place herself in a position to be laughed at—not a pleasant prospect for a lady so concerned about appearances. Painted boxes were often, in those days, love-gifts, and from the first moment he'd seen her with her friends, Vlemk had known that, even if he had in some sense once loved her, he could not say he loved her now and could hardly imagine recapturing that emotion, though some things about her—the tilt of her head—recalled it, teasingly and faintly, heightening the shock of their mutual change. And so, clearly, he had no business here, certainly no business offering a gift that, given in front of others, had nuances of insult and entrapment, as if one were to offer a lady a dead infant in its coffin, declaring it her own. Even if, as a professional painter of pictures on boxes, he could carry it off—avoid the implications of sentiment that displeased her—there was the matter of the box itself, or rather the picture: she, the imitation of the Princess, would not be happy

here, God knew. How much responsibility should one
have, he wondered, for a feeling creature that was not,
strictly speaking, a creature? Whatever the right answer,
the fact remained that feel she did, and her pain and
indignation were not easy matters to ignore. Even now
as he walked up the marble stairway, followed the Princess and her gathering friends down the long, blue-
carpeted, chandeliered hallway, and turned in, behind
her, to a room filled with mirrors and figures wrought
in gold — a room she had chosen, he recognized at once
(knowing her as he did) for the irony it imparted, an
irony that defused the effect of his coming and put limits
of a kind on the scene she feared (he had forgotten, of
course, that she was afraid of his art, afraid of the idea
of a painting so perfect it could smile or cry or talk,
though of course he had known it, had seen, while exploring her with his brush, that fear of what whimsy
might lead to, her terror in the face of the unexpected)
— even now, as he sat at the low glass table in the center
of the room, obedient to her command, the muffled voice
under the cloth was complaining, berating him, insulting the Princess.

"I want to go home," the tiny voice wailed. "You've
all gone crazy! I don't look like her at all!"

Vlemk raised his eyebrows, closed his eyes, and
pressed one finger down gently to stop the painted
mouth. He set the box on the table, still in its black velvet
cloth, and waited for the guests to gather and the Princess to take her place. It was not strictly true, apparently,
that the moustached young man had been too scrupu-
lous to read Vlemk's note. On every side of him Vlemk
could hear whispered speculations on whether or not

the painted picture would talk. At last a servant pulled
back the Princess's chair, his head bowed in the way
people bow when they quickly and casually say grace,
and the Princess seated herself, unsmilingly, opposite
Vlemk. When the room had quieted, Vlemk, with infinite weariness, scorning himself for this obedience to
mindless ritual but seeing no way out, boxed in by the
illusory infinity of mirrors, bent forward and removed
the black cloth. The Princess for an instant looked not
at the box but at Vlemk the box-painter, as if assuring
herself that, like her, he meant no harm. Then her gaze
dropped to the box, and she seemed to pale. The room
was faintly humming. After a moment she looked up
at the man at her left, the old servant. "Do I actually
look like that?" she asked quietly, her voice so sweet
that Vlemk's heart wrenched. The servant seemed to
muse, bending closer, two fingers on the corner of his
spectacles—for all one could tell, he was sincere and
honest. At last he said, "I'm not sure, your highness.
I don't really see the resemblance."

Vlemk smiled.

"Stupid, stupid, stupid," whispered the picture, making sure that no one heard but her maker.

Now the Princess was looking hard at Vlemk the
box-painter. "You say it talks?" she said.

"She talks if she wishes to," he wanted to say, but
being unable to speak, Vlemk simply nodded.

Then, to Vlemk's horror, the picture said crossly, with
undisguised contempt, "So you're the famous beautiful
Princess."

A gasp went through the room, and the Princess's
face went blank. People began whispering; here and

there someone laughed; others began shushing them for silence, hoping to hear more from the box. When everything was still again, the picture said:

"You find your image unflattering, Princess?" The painted face paused, waiting for full attention. "Perhaps you've been painted too often by people who 'respect' you." The picture smiled.

The Princess, to her credit, was as calm as stone. To Vlemk she said, "Is the picture always so insulting?"

Vlemk nodded, then in fairness shook his head, then shrugged. He rolled his eyes in the direction of the box and hoped that it would soon learn resignation and, if only for his sake, make peace.

At this moment there was a commotion, and, looking up, Vlemk saw — guided by the eyes of all the others — that on a balcony high on the wall behind him, a balcony he'd failed to notice before, a golden door was opening. After a moment a man in a wheelchair came carefully through the door, assisted beyond his need by eager servants. Vlemk knew the face at once, ravaged and sorrowful, infinitely patient yet capable of flying into rages over trifles, the face of a man of keen intelligence, plagued by some constant, nagging pain and bearing up as well as he's able. It was the king whose picture was on the coin. He seemed at death's door. His eyes were slits, his body so wasted, beneath the splendid clothes, that a small child might have carried him in her arms like a doll. He tipped his head — he wore no crown — as if gazing down at the company, then feebly waved his bejewelled hand as a sign that the business at hand, whatever it might be, should go on as before. The people bowed and bent their knees to him, some with tears in their eyes; he solemnly nodded back; and then, gradually, all eyes returned to the box.

The Princess said, "Vlemk, my friend, whatever the personality of this toy you've created, there can be no denying that you're an amazing painter of boxes. We accept your gift with pleasure."

Vlemk sadly nodded, ignoring the look of wild outrage from the box, the tiny wail of "Toy indeed!" If he closed his eyes, he knew he would see his friend the Princess as she'd looked that day when she'd refused, out of kindness, to throw him a coin from the carriage. All that was a long time ago, and Vlemk (so he told himself) had no regrets. Nevertheless, he was careful to keep his eyes open, and pressing his hands on the arms of the chair, he prepared to get up and leave.

But the picture on the box was not so pleased with the way things were going, and spoke again: "If you find me unflattering, you should look at the pictures in his studio. He's painted you again and again, Princess. Perhaps in one of the others you'd find something to your taste."

The strength went out of Vlemk's arms, and he sat as he was.

"Is this true?" asked the Princess, both interested and uneasy.

Like images in a nightmare, Vlemk's dreadful pictures of the Princess rose up before his eyes. It was not that he believed them false, exactly — indeed, the drooping eyelid he had predicted was now an actuality, at least when the Princess was angry. Nevertheless, the pictures were not things he desperately wanted her to see. He tried to think whether to nod or shake his head, and at last he pretended he hadn't heard her.

"I must admit," said the Princess almost apologetically, as if admitting that the fault might indeed be her own, "though I'm naturally impressed by the picture you've brought me, I'm not quite sure I see the likeness."

A noise came from the balcony, and instantly everyone looked up. "It speaks," cried the King in a wheedling, childish voice, banging his tiny fist on the arm of the wheelchair. "Think about that, girl! It's real enough to speak!" Instantly a terrible coughing fit took him, blood fell from his nose, and his servants rushed him—shuddering and shaking and snapping his teeth—from the room.

6

THOUGH SHE HADN'T ADMITTED IT the Princess was disturbed by the picture Vlemk had left her, and as the spring days passed her discomfort in its presence increased. She would have had it destroyed if she could bring herself to do so, but the thought nagged at her that facing the whole matter squarely might somehow be important. Moreover, the idea of destroying the picture, even when it attacked her with its vulgar little tongue, made her tremble with superstitious alarm. If she threw it in the fire, might that not be a kind of murder, even though the substance of the creature she destroyed was just paint? And there was this, though she hardly dared think of it: as the flames leaped up around the picture, destroying it, might not she suddenly feel an onslaught of mysterious heat—might she not, in fact. . . She refused to let the thought complete itself.

Sometimes, if she was lucky, she was able to catch the picture in its sleep, and could gaze at the image thoughtfully for long periods, as she could never have gazed at her image in the mirror, for then the eyes were of course always open and every flicker of thought was reflected, so that nothing was to be trusted, she could never get inside herself. It had struck her as true of many

people—the man with the moustache was only one—
that what they saw as most interesting or charming in
themselves was never in fact what was best in them:
their finest expressions, their most beautiful aspects,
were things unknown to them, because never shown in
any mirror. She could see that the man with the moustache for example—a Prince who was considered by
the kingdom's chief ministers to be an excellent match
—had been persuaded by his mirror that his noblest
expression was the one in which he lifted an eyebrow
in ironic amusement. Personally she found that super-
cilious look downright offensive. She could imagine how
tiresome and stupid it would look when he was eighty.
What drew the Princess's heart to the man—despite
her displeasure at being treated as a brood mare, an
ambush piece in a political chess game, was the look
of childish bafflement that sometimes came over him,
a look she was sure he'd never seen on himself and
would have done almost anything to avoid.

Though at first she'd been convinced that the box-
painter's image was nothing at all like her—a surpris-
ing lapse in the box-painter's art or a proof that his
manner of living had done damage to his brain—she
had gradually begun to revise her opinion, examining
the image when the eyes were closed. She saw blue lights
in the temples that vaguely frightened her: she was more
mortal than she thought. She saw, in addition to the
many things that pleased her, little troublesome hints
of cruelty, vanity, and stinginess. She began to think
the portrait was accurate, and she was filled with a feeling like moths fluttering in her chest.

It was worse, of course, when the picture on the box

was awake. It would sit watching her, smug as a cat, or it would say things she never would have dreamed of saying, that is, things she would never have said to herself even in a dream. By the slightest twist of a phrase, the picture on the box could make her heart turn ice. The most innocent remark—"You do have your little ways, don't you?"—spoken in her own unmistakable voice (unmistakable to her), with her own secret ironies ringing down and down, could emotionally disable the Princess for a week. Her anguish at such moments was so baffling and complex she could hardly make out what it was that she felt, she could only go to bed and weep. What the box said to her was for one thing so infuriatingly stupid, which meant, she knew, that she, the Princess, was for all her fine airs stupid, tiresome, in fact worthless. Though she was outwardly young, the tedious clichés with which the box attacked her—her own clichés, her own forms of attack—revealed to her that nothing was any longer new about her, the prettily painted box might as well have been her casket. At the same time, what the box said was true, however monstrously unfair—undeniably true. The picture on the box hated her; that was the gist of it. She hated herself. She needed healing, needed the touch of some loving magician who would transform her, return her to her childhood innocence, but who could love her?, and if anyone did—the Prince, for example— could an intelligent woman give her heart to such a fool? There were plenty all around her who were willing to give her praise, plenty to whom she could play the Good Princess like a skillful actress, hating herself all the more as she played the role. But there was no one who could silence the voice of the truth-telling box. Even when the picture on the box was quiet, like a watchful animal, a murderer biding his time, it seemed to the Princess that it could fill all the high, square room with its crackling contempt. The picture hated her; if that was all there was to it, she would have been ruined, and that would have been that.

But the picture on the box had another side to it. Sometimes it spoke its emotions without thinking, forgetting its hatred and simply responding to the warmth of the sunlight pouring through the window, the music of the songbirds, or the beauty of the wheatfields sloping away toward the river to the west of the palace. She, the Princess, would feel herself splaying anew to the warmth of the summer, or noticing again, as she hadn't in years, how lovely the wheatfields were, yellowing into season. That voice too, the voice that gave her unthinking and unstinting praise, was unmistakably her own, and the Princess was in those moments as pleased with herself—however briefly and unsurely—as a child who's been given some wonderful gift for no reason.

The feeling was not all sweetness. It inevitably heightened in the Princess's mind the disparity between what she felt to be her best self and knew to be her worst. One day, for instance, walking in the garden with the Prince who wore the moustache, pointing out to him the glow of a blooming tea rose, she was suddenly overwhelmed by anxiety, wondering which was the truer feeling, the innocent delight which had sprung the remark or the manipulative instinct that had turned it to a ploy in their game of political-romantic *rapprochement*.

"As lovely as your eyes," said the Prince, idiotically.

"Are my eyes red, then?" asked the Princess, lowering her lashes and giving him a smile.

"I was really thinking of your cheeks," said the Prince, with that look of childish bafflement and embarrassment she usually liked on him. Today she was only annoyed by it — annoyed partly, if she told herself the truth, by the virginal innocence it revealed in him, an innocence she could not match. "Is it not true," she asked herself angrily, "that the Prince's remark *was* stupid and manipulative?—aesthetically stupid, a floundering metaphor, and both politically and sexually manipulative: Why should a woman's cheeks (or eyes) be celebrated for their redness, as would a child's, and not a man's?"— for her Prince would be insulted beyond words, she knew, if she should seek to flatter him by praise of his pretty, red cheeks. (They *were* red, in fact, and for a manic instant she thought of trying it.) Yet alas, both the stupidity and the attempt at manipulation came bubbling from the Prince in the moustache as innocently as water from a well, as unconsidered and open-hearted as grapes on a grapevine or pink and blue hollyhocks blooming beside a farmer's brick house.

"Are you all right?" asked the Prince with a look of alarm. Her face was flushed — as red as a rose, he might have said if he'd thought of it — and for no clear reason there were tears in her eyes.

"My dear, dear Princess," he said, in panic now, "is it something I said?"

"It's nothing," said the Princess, and put the tips of her fingers to her forehead.

"Perhaps we'd better go inside," said the Prince, and

gave an irritable glance up past his shoulder, as if the heavens' overbrightness were at fault.

"Yes, perhaps we'd better," the Princess said.

At the door to her room they parted with a touch of hands, the Princess promising to be out again soon, as soon as she'd had a little rest. The minute the door was closed, she hurried to her bed and lay down with her head on the pillow, one hand draped limply across her forehead.

The picture on the box was feeling talkative. "Have a nice time?" it asked, ironically putting on the voice of an old woman.

At once, in a fury, the Princess sat up again.

"Not the quilt! Not the quilt!" cried the picture— for of late it was the Princess's habit to cover the box with a heavy yellow quilt in hopes of silencing it. "I'll be good! I'll be nothing but sweetness and light! You have my promise!"

The Princess lay back again and closed her eyes, not resting, ready to spring if the box started in again.

After a long time the box asked, trying to sound innocent, "Did he talk dirty?"

The Princess groaned.

"It's not that I *mean* to be troublesome," said the picture hastily, thinking of the quilt. "And of course it's none of my business what your suitors say to you. It's just that life's not very interesting for a person who's not real, if you know what I mean. Has it ever occurred to you that all I have is a head and neck and shoulders? I can't even play with my—"

"Stop it!" cried the Princess, sitting up again. "Where in heaven's name do you get those vulgar, obscene, unspeakable . . ." She did not finish, but put her hands to her face and bent forward like a person in pain. "Why do you hate me?" she whispered. "What is it you *want* of me?"

"I don't hate you, really," said the picture, then abruptly went silent, thinking her own thoughts.

After a long time the Princess said, "You told me once that Vlemk the box-painter made other pictures of me."

The picture on the box let the sentence hang in the air a moment, then brought out, in a voice strangely quiet, "Yes . . ."

"What are they like?" the Princess asked.

The picture on the box said nothing.

"Well?" asked the Princess.

"You'd have to see them," said the picture, again in that quiet, reserved voice that might mean anything.

"Perhaps I will," said the Princess thoughtfully, and dropped her hands to her knees, one hand on the other, her eyes staring vacantly at the farther wall. After a moment she said, "I'm told the box-painter is very poor. Perhaps if I went with a few friends to his shop, people who could afford to pay him well if he happened to have something that struck their fancy . . ."

Again the picture on the box said nothing.

"I don't mean we'd give him charity," said the Princess. It's just that, I thought . . ."

The picture on the box said, "I'm sorry I don't please you. I don't blame you for being angry, I've been thinking of no one but myself, I admit it. Perhaps if we both could try harder — especially me, I mean —"

The Princess frowned. "You don't *want* me to see the other boxes!"

"Oh, it isn't that!" the picture exclaimed. But the Princess knew her own voice too well to be fooled.

"That settles it!" said the Princess. She rose quickly and crossed to the door to call a servant and send a message to her driver. The Prince, who had been standing with his hands behind his back, looking at the pictures of nobility on the walls, saw the Princess talking with her servant and came to greet her.

"Are you better, then?" he asked.

"Prince!" she said, giving him a quick, false smile. "I've thought of something we must do. Will you help me?"

"Anything at all, my love," said the Prince, and shifted his eyes to some point above her head, slightly troubled by that smile.

"We must do something to help the poor box-painter," she said. "There he is living in abject poverty, though he may well be one of the most brilliant artists in the kingdom!" And she told him her plan.

7

A WHISPER WENT through the tavern, and the next thing Vlemk the box-painter knew, the barmaid was leaning down to him, murmuring in his ear. Though he did not quite hear what she said, he turned around and, there at the doorway, saw the man who drove the Princess's carriage, dressed in all his finery, with the boots that shone like onyx.

Vlemk's mind was beclouded—he'd drunk a good deal of wine—and he turned to his friends in hopes of judging by their faces what was wanted of him. The poet was asleep with his eyes rolled up; the axe-murderer was staring dully straight ahead, like a man in a trance. "He's asking to see *you*," said the ex-violinist, and jabbed his long finger in the direction of the carriage driver. Vlemk looked up at the barmaid. She nodded.

Slowly, clumsily, Vlemk felt for and found his shoes —which he'd pulled out of because of the pain they gave him—scuffed his feet into them, and struggled to get up out of his seat. The barmaid took his arm, helping him, saying in his ear, "Don't be afraid! I think it's something good!" and led him across the room to where the carriage driver waited, aloof and displeased by everything around him—the open mouths, warts, and blemishes of the regulars, the stink of stale whiskey, sickness, and tobacco, the barmaid's tomcat lying over by the bar on his back, his eyes rolled sideways, waiting for someone to drop food. As Vlemk approached, the driver gave a kind of smile and a bow that was almost obsequious but constrained, full of grim reservations.

"The Princess," said the driver, "has asked if you might possibly be willing to open your shop."

Vlemk opened his mouth, put his hand on his chin, and thought deeply.

"She is interested in looking at your work," said the driver.

After a time, Vlemk nodded. He felt for the top of his head, seeing if his hat was there, then nodded again. He sensed some awful trouble outside the door, but his drunkenness was unable to place it, and so, at length, he nodded again and moved with the driver toward the entrance.

Outside, four carriages were lined up, filled with people. Vlemk removed his hat. The door of the black and gold carriage opened, and the Princess leaned out to smile at him. "Hello, Vlemk. I'm sorry we weren't sure about your hours."

Vlemk laughed, then stopped himself, thoughtfully licked his lips, then nodded. "No matter," he tried to say, then remembered the curse and simply shrugged.

"Would you do us the honor of riding with us?" asked the Princess.

He gazed at her in dismay, looked up and down the street, then helplessly shrugged again. With his hat in his hands he moved toward the carriage and, when he reached it, raised one foot, like a blind man. The driver bent down beside him and guided the foot to the shining

brass step, then gently helped him in. He could see nothing inside the carriage—he had a sense of white faces
gazing at him like moons—and had no choice but to
submit to their kindness as they turned him and aimed
his rear end toward the seat beside the Princess. "Thank
you," said the Princess, leaning past him; and the driver
closed the door.

"It's a great honor to meet you again," said a voice
Vlemk faintly recognized. A glowing white hand hung
in front of him, and after a moment he understood that
he was meant to shake it. Clumsily, he did so, then
wiped his hand on his trousers. The carriage smelled
of flowers or perfume. Vlemk breathed very shallowly
for fear of being sick.

"It's a fortunate kingdom," said another voice, "that
has artists of such stature and renown!"

"Renown is for gargoyle hackers," Vlemk said scorn-
fully; but luckily no sound came out. His hands lay on
his knees. The Princess's glove came down gently on the
hand to the right. He was puzzled to find it shaking
like the hand of a madwoman.

The carriage swayed, soundless as a boat on the water
except for the tocking of the horses' iron shoes on the
cobblestones, rhythmical as clocks. Then the sound
stopped and, soon after, the swaying also stopped, and
the door at Vlemk's elbow fell open. He caught his
breath, but all was well. The driver was extending his
hand.

It was while he was climbing the stairs that his mind
came back to him. A shock went through him, and he
glanced down past his arm at the lords and ladies following him up the steps in all their finery. They were

smiling like children at a party, expecting presents, and with a turn of the stomach he realized what it was they'd come for, what it was they wanted to see. Without his willing it, his feet stopped and his left hand clamped tight on the bannister as if never to be moved. The Princess, just behind him, looked up at his face inquiringly, waiting, dark circles under her eyes, and after a moment, touching his beard, wetting his lips, Vlemk continued climbing.

As he lighted the candles in his studio the box-painter hesitated again, wondering if perhaps he might fool them by keeping the place relatively dark. But it was not to be, for the Prince with the moustache, ever eager to be useful, had found phosphor sticks and was hurrying here and there through the studio finding more candles in their old china dishes and lighting them, one after another. Soon the place was glowing like a room in the palace, and Vlemk knew that all was lost. Slowly, deliberately, he brought the little boxes from their various places—first the shoddily painted boxes with landscapes on them, then the boxes with flowers, then the boxes with cats and dogs—but he knew from the beginning that it would not be enough. He stood with his hands in his pockets and his eyes half closed, like some pot-bellied watchman asleep on his feet, and observed as they admired those shameless betrayals of his gift.

"I had heard, . . ." said the Princess, and let the words trail off.

She seemed to Vlemk very young, very frightened, just an ordinary child, not a Princess whose father, though said to be dying, had powers like a god's in this kingdom. The Prince with the moustache stood beside her, his hand on her arm, as childlike as the girl, in the painter's eyes, a cocky, good-looking boy who'd never seen trouble, had no idea—unless he'd gotten it from books or the tales of old servants—that in the streets below there were axe-murderers, people who picked pockets, men who crept like rats through cloakrooms. He could say, he thought—that is, he could manage to impart to them by gestures—that he had no more boxes, that the pictures she'd heard of did not exist. But he saw that again she was shaping the question, opening her mouth to speak, and he did not have it in him, he found, to lie to her. He retained, despite his efforts, too much of that original lunatic vision, the shadowy reality peeking out from behind what she was.

Vlemk the box-painter nodded grimly, and brought out the boxes on which he'd painted all her worst potential. When he'd displayed them he turned curtly and went over to stand with his back to them, looking out the window. It occurred to him briefly that he might jump from it, but he was too old, too familiar with misery to be moved by cheap romance. He heard them whispering. No, they were not pleased.

"How tragic!" someone whispered.

Vlemk nodded grimly and smiled to himself. He had forgotten their talent for self-delusion. He put on a doltish look, turned back to them, and opened his hands as if to ask, "What do you think?"

"Beautiful! Just beautiful!" said a lady with silver hair. "How much?"

Vlemk ignored her, watching the Princess. Her lips faintly trembled and she shot a quick look at him, something between bafflement and anger. Then she looked down again. The picture on the box she was holding in her hand was one he called, privately, "The Princess Considers Revenge." If anyone had cared to look, it was her mirror image now, the face distorted, short of breath, the lips slightly puffy, the eyes sharp and stupid as an animal's. Eager to press the scene to its conclusion, Vlemk shrugged so broadly, with a look so unspeakably foolish, that the Princess could not help but look up at him. "What do you think?" he asked again with his hands and arms.

She stared straight at him, guessing, he suspected, that he was putting on some act.

"I don't like it," the Princess said. "I don't think I look like that."

A stillness went through them all. She had given them permission to despise him.

"It's true," said the lady with the silver hair, looking at the box she'd just admired, "it's not a good likeness, really."

They looked at each other. Vlemk went on grinning like a fool and waiting. Only the Prince in the moustache seemed not to have noticed what had happened. He was staring with interest at a small, meticulously painted little pill box on which the Princess was shown waking from a dream of terrible debauchery. He turned it slightly — it was no larger around than a coin — making the glaze of the lips catch the light. "I like this one," he said, and held it toward the Princess, then saw her face.

"You should buy it," she said, cold as ice.

The poor boy had no notion of what it was he'd done wrong. His hand lowered as if all strength had suddenly drained out of his arm, and he looked again, critically and sadly at the picture. The fact, Vlemk saw, was that he *did* like it, that his innocent heart saw no evil in it, and rightly enough, because for him there was no evil there. "I don't know," he said, and his innocence was, that instant, just a little corrupted. He compressed his lips, as if he dimly understood himself what it was that was happening to him; but he was weak, without defenses, and after another quick look at the others, put the box back down on the table where he'd found it, "No," he said, "I guess not. I don't know."

The Princess had turned toward the door. She stood thinking, her features completely expressionless, the look of a woman taking pains to hide her thoughts. Her small fingers picked irritably at her clothes. Vlemk the box-painter, who knew every muscle and bone in that lovely young face, was not thrown for a moment. She would turn — she turned — and would reach almost at random for a painted box, almost certainly a landscape — she reached for a landscape — and would hold it up to ask "How much?"

The Princess looked up, seemed to hesitate an instant, as if reading something in Vlemk's eyes. "How much?" she asked.

Vlemk put on a sad, apologetic look and told her in gestures that unfortunately that one was not for sale. She moved instantly, like a chess player who knows her opponent, putting the box down and picking up another one, not even looking at it. "This one?" she asked sharply.

He must have shown surprise. He covered as quickly as possible; it was better to take her charity than to continue this dangerous game. He raised six fingers, then with one finger and his thumb made a circle the size of the coin with the king on it—an exorbitant price.

Her eyes widened in astonishment, then suddenly she laughed, and then, just as suddenly, she shot him a hard, inquiring look. That too she quickly veiled, lowering her lashes. "Very well, six crowns," she said, and gestured to her servant, who reached with clumsy haste into his purse.

The lady with silver hair was at once struck by another of his landscapes; a gentleman in a wig found himself drawn to a picture of two dogs. The Prince in the moustache let his eyes wander over in the direction of the picture he'd been taken by, then thought better of it and began to look with studious interest at pictures of flowers. Vlemk waited until everyone was occupied, bending over landscapes, flowers, and animals, then slipped "The Dream of Debauchery" from its place, waited for his moment, slapped the Princess on the arm in the age-old pick-pocket's way, and dropped the little pillbox into his pocket.

"How much?" they asked, one after another. "How much?"

Each price he quoted, holding up his fingers, was more outrageous than the last. The Princess eyed him coolly, then went over to stand at the window, lost in thought. When it was time for them to leave, the Princess smiled, somewhat falsely, and said, "Good luck, Vlemk. God be with you, you poor man."

"A touch!" said Vlemk inside his mind, taking her hand and kissing it. "A touch! I felt it right here, just under my heart!"

8

HOWEVER, the Princess was not yet rid of those evil-hearted pictures her friend the box-painter had made. Studying the picture that could talk, in her room, she was more and more convinced that her father had been right. It was indeed her true likeness, much as she hoped it might not be. Might not the others, still less pleasing, be equally true to what she was? She tried to summon them up in her mind, but her memory was fuzzy, or if not, some mechanism distorted the image as soon as it came to her, burned it as an image is burned out of clarity when one looks at it in too much light.

"Why did he paint them, I wonder?" she asked aloud one day, standing at her window, talking to herself.

"I'm sure he meant no harm," said the picture on the box, its voice no louder than the buzzing of a bee.

The Princess tipped her head, not quite turning to the box. After a moment she asked, "Does he hate me, do you think. Is that it?"

"He never spoke of you unkindly, so far as I remember," said the picture on the box.

"You're lying," said the Princess, though in fact she was not sure. For some queer reason she found it harder and harder to know what the image on the box was thinking, even when the tone of voice was most distinctly her own.

"I'm not!" said the picture with a touch of indignation. "The fact is, I never heard him mention you!"

"Well he certainly must have given me some
thought," said the Princess. "I mean, my face seems
to be an obsession with him!"

"Ah!" said the picture. "So you admit that there is
indeed some slight resemblance!"

"I admit nothing!" snapped the Princess. "Stop quiz-
zing me!" Quickly, to avoid further argument, she left
the room.

But her doubts would not leave her a moment's peace.
Sitting at supper, with the Prince across from her, looking gloomy because he no longer understood her and
the time of his visit was nearing its end, the matter
between them still entirely unresolved, the Princess,
taking a small bite of her roll, would suddenly see Vlemk
the box-painter's image of her eating a piece of chicken
with a look of insatiable gluttony, her eyes like a
weasel's. Or walking in the woods, wringing her hands
and tossing her hair back again and again, as if to drive
away fierce thoughts or deny unfounded charges made
by people she had trusted implicitly, she would suddenly
see in her mind's eye, more real than the ferns and trees
around her, Vlemk the box-painter's image of her tearing at her cheeks with her fingernails, gone mad.

One night her father the king came into her room,
something he had never done before. When the door
was closed behind him and his servants had stepped back
in the way he required of them, seeming to disappear
like September mist into the curtains and walls, the
king, clutching at his clothes with a kind of unconscious
desperation, as if anything that touched him, any slight-

est physicality, gave him a scalding pain, almost more than he could bear, raised his head with great difficulty and said: "Daughter, what's the matter with you? I'm told on good authority you're like a woman that's out of her wits."

The Princess went white with fear, for like everyone in the palace she had experience of her father's rages.

"Don't lie!" snapped her father.

"I wasn't going to!" she snapped back, indignant.

His eyebrows lifted, and he studied her, his tiny claws pulling more fiercely at his clothes. "Good," he said. His head snapped back suddenly, as if something invisible had struck him on the chin, and he shook all over, his hands flying out over the wheelchair arms, fluttering like wings, until the fit was over. The servants stood like monkeys, bent forward, prepared to rush to him. When he could raise his head again, sweat streaming down onto his nose and beard, he said, "Tell me what's the matter, then. I haven't much time left—as any damn fool can see." When she said nothing, he said, "Well?"

"I haven't been myself," said the Princess feebly. She noticed, in horror, that she was picking at the front of her dress, exactly as her father did, though not so wildly.

His head fell toward her, tilted sideways, the lips stretched wide with agony. "Don't waste time!" he cried. "Have mercy!" Again, more violently than before, the old king's head shot back and the trembling came over him. The servants moved toward him, and— with such strength of will that the Princess was thrown into awe of him—his fluttering hands waved them back. "No time for niceties!" he gasped. His nose began to bleed and he tried to take an angry swipe at it.

It was the box that cried out in an agony of love and sorrow, "Tell him! For the love of God tell him and be done with it!"

The king rolled his eyes toward the box, then let them fall upward again.

"Very well!" the Princess said, clutching at her dress, twisting and wrinkling it, then straightening it again. In a rush, she told him all. When she was finished, she sat staring at her knees, weeping and occasionally sniffing, jerking back her head.

The king let his head and shoulders fall forward, his eyelids sinking over his eyes as if by their weight. With what seemed his last breath, he said, "Go to the box-painter. Beg him to remove the curse. Otherwise we're doomed."

"Princess!" cried the picture on the box in a voice unlike any the Princess had ever heard from it, "he's dying! Run to him!"

Without thinking, the Princess obeyed. "Father!" she cried, "Father, for the love of God!" Now the servants were all around her, and it seemed to the Princess in her madness that the walls of the room had caught fire.

"Don't die!" she whispered, but she knew now, flames all around her, that that was why he'd come to her. In the ferocious heat, it was as if her mind had flown open and she knew everything everyone in the room was thinking. Then, the next instant, in the blinding whiteness, her mind went blank.

"Princess," one of the servants said softly, lifting her as if she weighed nothing, "we'll take care of him. Rest yourself."

Slowly, the illusion of fire sank away, and she was standing, supported by servants, gazing at something too still, too full of peace to be her father. Now his strange words came back to her: "Beg him to remove the curse."

The day after the king was buried, she went to the box-painter.

9

SHE COULD NOT BELIEVE, at first, the change that had
come over him. He seemed much older, much sadder,
so gentle that the Princess (she would not officially be
Queen until New Year's Day) could almost have believed
she had dreamed their last meeting, when he'd charged
those mad prices for the worthless pictures she and
her friends had bought, carelessly scrawled landscapes
of cows crossing streams, sickly, drab asphodels and
forget-me-nots, day lilies and primroses, or those
maudlin little animals, cats, dogs, teddy bears — not so
much box-paintings as angry parodies, at best, of the
box-painter's art. He was busy at the same kinds of
subjects now, but with such a difference that they
seemed not the work of the same hand. His paintings
of gardens were so accurate in each detail, even to the
occasional weed or insect, so alive with the spirit of
whoever it was that had planted them — some old
woman, she imagined, or some old man in suspenders,
once a farmer or a lawyer, who'd settled down in his
final days to make the life he was leaving more comfortable for someone he knew, or perhaps did not know,
for the world in general, with all its sorrows — so accurate in its depiction of both the beauty and sadness of
the world as it is, that one believed, if one closed one's
eyes, that one could smell the autumn leaves.

Nor was the studio he worked in the same at all. What had seemed a kind of crypt never visited except by the artist's ghost, a bleak place of weariness, misery, and failure, had now become a hive of activity. There were customers who greedily sorted through the boxes, pretending to find fault with them to get an easier price, children and old people, a lean, smiling banker with a terrible worried look flickering around his eyes—he was looking for a box for his wife, he said, and had no idea what might appeal to her ("Bring her in!" said the box-painter with gestures, "Bring her in!"), an angry old woman, a laborer, a midget. . . . Vlemk the box-painter had taken on three young apprentices, two dull, lanky ones and one who was fat and near-sighted— "A master!" Vlemk told her with gestures, "a genius!" She looked at the young man with distaste: plump, pink-cheeked, working with his tongue between his teeth, bending down to watch, almost cross-eyed, as his mallet ticked brads into the eight-sided box he was at work on. When he saw that she was watching he smiled and gave her a wink that seemed vaguely obscene. Quickly, she looked away. How Vlemk had done it all in less than a month was a mystery to her, for the Princess had no idea that she herself was at the heart of the change. Her friends who'd bought boxes had made Vlemk the social *dernier cri*, and they had done so just at the moment when, as chance would have it, he was in a mood to revise his life. That too was of course her influence, though she could not know it. She could know only that he was a changed man, an artist again, though not at all the artist she had come to seek out—and in fact not an artist she approved of. There had been in him,

before, something scornful and majestic, the dignity
and barely contained rage of a fallen Lucifer, a haughty
detachment, unbending pride, even in his abject poverty, that transformed his afflictions, even his muteness,
to bends of nobility. Now overnight he had become just
another peasant artisan — indeed, a man at ease with
peasant artisans: over by the window, timidly peering
down with tiny pig's eyes through his thick, thick spectacles, stood a famous stained-glass-window maker
called Lefs — her father had often been his patron —
and on a stool, half-asleep, sat Borm the bell-maker, a
thick-nosed, doltish looking fellow with hair in his ears.

She stood erect, her face half hidden in the cave of
her hood, her gloved hand closed on the doorknob. She
was half inclined to flee, sick at heart. It was at that
moment, looking around her at the tedious goodness
that rolled like granulating honey through the box-
painter's shop (such was her word for it; she was no
longer comfortable calling it a studio), that the Princess
understood that the terrible paintings of her were true.
She might not like it, she might — knees trembling —
feel shocked toward despair by the frightening fact, but
she knew that those paintings she had seen were serious,
as none of this was, that the mind that had seared
through her flesh to the bones, the mind that with the
icy indifference of a god, had layer after layer torn the
sham away, the childish eagerness, the ridiculous pre-
tenses — the mind that had stripped her and used her
and dismissed her — was the mind, sublime and cold-
blooded, of an artist. Tears sprang to her eyes as she
considered the ruin he had become: a man worth, once,
all the gold in the kingdom, a thousand kingdoms, now

reduced, without even knowing it, to this. She remembered with incredulity how once she had refused to let a coin be tossed to him, imagining in her madness that it might lead him to "further debauchery!" Unconsciously she raised her hand to her eyes. The movement was enough to draw the attention of Vlemk the box-painter.

At once he came toward her, moving his lips in some remark of dismay, as if he'd forgotten that he'd lost the gift of speech.

"I must go," she said, and opened the door. A warm breath presaging rain came in.

Grotesquely, solicitous as her moustached Prince, he caught the edge of the door, half closed it, and held it. He gestured and rolled his eyes. Heaven knew what he was saying. His gaze was fixed on her black band of mourning.

"I must go," she said again, this time more sternly.

A calm came over him. A coldness, rather; faintly reminiscent of his greater days. With the look of a man killing an insect while holding a conversation—a brief wince, then no change in his expression—he closed the door. She stared, a little frightened, trying to read his eyes. He simply stood there, queerly smiling, the hum of sweetness filling the room behind him, customers chattering, his apprentices hurrying, now painting, now talking, no one noticing the two of them—herself and Vlemk, as removed as two stars. She jerked at the doorknob. She might as well have jerked at a knob on a wall of stone. She focused on the doorknob, studying the wild leap of feeling inside her. She was angry enough to scream at him, but at the center of her rage lay the mad question: Am I in love with this pot-bellied old man?

"I'll come back when you're less busy," she said.

"You've come to see the pictures," he said. Though she knew it was impossible, he seemed to say it with his voice.

"Yes I have," she said.

Vlemk the box-painter nodded, polite, then took his hand from the door and turned away. He stopped to speak in gestures to one of his apprentices — the young man looked over at the Princess, then quickly back at Vlemk — then, half-smiling, nodding to his customers, stepping carefully past his table of boxes, the box-painter went to a covered stack in the corner of the room, lifted off the cover, took a folded sack from the floor beside them, and indifferently dropped the boxes, one by one, into the sack. When he returned to her, the box-painter took her hand as he would a child's, hardly looking at her, opened the door, led her from the room, and softly pulled the door closed behind them. Then, letting go of her hand, he started down the stairway. The Princess followed.

Strange as it may seem, the Princess had never before seen the inside of a tavern. She walked with the false assurance of a blind man pretending he needs no help, pressing forward, stiff and erect, waiting as if impatiently for Vlemk to choose a table, though in fact she had no idea whether or not it was accepted practice for a man and woman to be seated together in a tavern. She was assaulted by such sensations, such newness and mystery, that she could hardly think, could only see and see, drinking in vision with the wide eyes of a child — indeed, she thought instantly of the way she had seen things at four or five, every surface alive, unnaturally sharp-edged: she remembered when she'd gone to the Fair with her father, servants all around them, looking out with sharp, fearful eyes for anarchists, her father still strong and tall, almost fat, crying "Ho, ho, ho" and shaking hands with his people when he could reach past the circle of guards.

The room was still, the people all pretending not to look at her. She stood, chin lifted, feeling a strange thrill of evil in her veins. What would people say?, she wondered, knowing what they'd say, and an image from one of Vlemk's paintings rose before her, what she secretly called "The Princess as Fallen Woman."

Then the barmaid stood beside them, more innocent than the Princess had been even in childhood, or so the Princess imagined, the barmaid companionably nodding and smiling, guiding them to a long table close to the front door, a table with candles on it, alongside it, six stolid chairs. Vlemk led the Princess to a chair by the wall, went back around the table to the chair directly opposite, and laid the sack on the table while the barmaid silently moved the other four chairs away. Vlemk made a signal, presumably his order, and the barmaid left. Then, without expression, Vlemk opened the sack and took out the boxes, one by one, and slid them across to her. When he'd removed the last box, he folded the sack and put it on his lap like a napkin. He splashed open his hands and smiled disparagingly, eyes remote. The Princess looked down at them.

It was incredible to her that they'd so shocked her the first time she'd seen them. There they were, her possibilities, each more terrible than the last; but they did not seem to her terrible now. It was like reading history books: this king died in battle, this king of syphilis, this one by a fall from his horse. What she felt, more than anything else, was a sense of new freedom, release. It was true, she thought, as if responding to something the talking picture on the box had said to her; this decorous life she'd pursued all her days was trivial, ludicrous. How strange and wonderful to be able to gaze down from the mountaintop, like a soul at last free of its body, and see life as it was. This king died in battle, this one of syphilis. . . .

One of the pictures showed her face tipped so high it seemed her neck would snap. "The Princess Full of Pride," she secretly named it. She laughed. Vlemk the box-painter glanced at her, judgmental, and she laughed again, more openly than she'd meant to. A man with yellow-white flaxen hair and sleepy eyes stopped abruptly in the middle of the room to look at her, then after a moment drew up a chair and sat down beside her. At just that moment the barmaid returned with the drinks Vlemk had ordered, two small, crude glasses that contained something thick and vaguely black. The barmaid looked daggers at the man who had come to sit with her, then looked questioningly at Vlemk, who lowered his eyes and shrugged. With a frightened expression, the barmaid glanced at the Princess. "It's no harm," said the Princess, and mimicked Vlemk's shrug. One casual hand raised to hide her ugly birthmark, the barmaid looked again at Vlemk, who pretended not to notice, then, at last, reluctantly turned away to go about her business.

"Hello," said the man with flaxen hair, and grinned

one-sidedly. His teeth were discolored and tilted, like headstones in an old, old graveyard.

She nodded and glanced at his patched, ragged elbow, too close to her own.

"I," said the man, "am a poet." He tipped his head back, slightly to one side, letting it sink in.

"That's nice," she said, and glanced at Vlemk. He was looking at the boxes. She too looked down at them.

"Poets are much disparaged in this moron age," said the poet.

She said nothing, but gave him a noncommittal nod and reached for a candle to give the boxes more light. The poet leaned closer, looking too. She lowered her eyebrows and tensed her forehead, straining to ignore him.

It seemed that any one of the paintings might speak if it wished to, even the ones done most carelessly, as if in disgust. What had he been thinking as he painted them?, she wondered again. And how was it that he could sit there so calmly now, two fingers around the stem of his glass, hardly looking at her, beginning to show signs of impatience. She drew away from the poet a little, shooting him a look, and then glanced again at Vlemk. Here in the tavern, with the candlelight making his graying hair glow like newly cut iron, he no longer seemed just one more artisan. In comparison to the poet, he might have been made of solid marble. "I have come to beg you to remove the curse," she thought of saying, and quickly looked down, driving out the image of her father by saying to herself with intense concentration, "It makes no sense."

The poet said, "Your eyes are like curdled cream. Does that offend you?"

She looked at him as she'd have looked at some curious insect.

Instantly, the poet rolled his eyes up and waggled his hands.

He looked exactly like her father, and the breath went out of her. She threw a wild glance at Vlemk for help, but Vlemk had his eyes closed, infinitely patient, burying both the poet and herself in the rot of time. Suddenly she found herself shaking like a machine, and Vlemk opened his eyes. He looked at the poet, so calmly that the whole world changed for her. Yes, she must learn to be like Vlemk the box-painter. Learn to dismiss with absolute indifference the antics of mere mortals! She must live for the imperishable! She'd been wrong about him, she saw now. He had not mellowed, gone soft. In the end he had dismissed even rage and scorn, even the young artist's hunger for truth. He had moved beyond silence to a terrible kind of comedy, painting nonsense with unholy skill—landscapes, animals, all that dying humanity foolishly clings to.

That instant Vlemk leaned forward, one finger raised as if in warning, and with a stern expression shook his head. Was he reading her mind? she wondered. He must be, of course. He knew her as no one had ever known her before, every spasm and twitch.

The boxes gleamed in the candlelight, a coolly disinterested catalogue of horrors—wretched grimaces, rolled eyes; ten obscene masks of corruption. And it came to her suddenly that the point was *not* that one of them was fated to come true: *all* of them were true. And it was not that he loved her or hated her. She was a specimen, simply, like the rat the biologist happens to come down on with his glove. He could have done it as well with the poet—she could do it herself, if she had his craft! This is the world, he had said. So much for the world! And he'd gone back to painting pretty gardens, where weeds pushed up, merry as crocuses, and insects chewed and were chewed, like gargoyles on a church. This is the world, my children, my moustached Princes, coyly smiling ladies. Again Vlemk's eyes were closed, burying all that lived. *I never heard him mention you*, the picture that could talk had said. Even when he was painting her hour after hour, he'd given her no more thought than the biologist gives to the frog he is cutting to pieces, still alive. That was Art. That was the mountaintop. The boxes blurred together in an image of her father's dying face.

She leaned forward, clutching the table, struggling to clear her sight. Her wits reeled, though she hadn't yet tasted the vaguely black drink. She found herself staring now at one of the boxes in particular—perhaps she'd been staring for some time. "The Princess Envious," she thought it might be called. It showed her face almost comically narrowed and peaked, her eyes enormous, the tips of her teeth showing.

Vlemk opened his eyes. "Your health," he said soundlessly, murderously ironic—or so it seemed to the Princess—and raised his glass.

Soon there were two more of them, friends of Vlemk, or so they claimed, and Vlemk accepted it in silence, eyelids sinking again. One maintained he was an ex-violinist. The other maintained nothing at all, staring at her throat a moment, occasionally glancing at the door as if expecting more of these "friends." The Prin-

cess could hardly breathe. All her life she had scorned
and avoided vulgarity, ugliness: but here, sunk deep in
both, she was revising her opinions. She had wanted
gardens without insects. She wanted that no longer. She
wanted now only to *see*. But her mind was fuzzy. She
strained for concentration. There was no feeling in the
tips of her fingers.

The poet said things so foolish one had to think about
them.

"Suppose," he said, floating his head toward her,
half moons of yellow below his irises, "suppose God
were a spider!"

She waited. He seemed to have nothing more to say.
But when she turned to the ex-violinist for help, the
poet broke in quickly, seizing the floor again, violently
trembling, "Out of his own *entrails* the spider spins!"
He gave a jerk, trying to raise his arm to shake his fist
at her, but his elbow struck hard against the edge of the
table, making him yelp and bringing tears to his eyes.
The ex-violinist shook his head and said, "Listen—"
Furiously, wildly, the poet struck out with his left narrow arm, hitting the ex-violinist in the chest. "But also
the spider stings!" the poet yelled. The voice, thin and
high, reminded her of the voice of the picture that could
talk, and abruptly she remembered that the picture was
herself. She looked at Vlemk. He was asleep.

The poet, for no reason, was crying. Softly, the ex-
violinist said, "He's so full of hate, this man. Who can
blame him?"

She looked for help at the man who sat staring at
her throat. Something in his look made her blood curdle,
and, smiling nervously, lowering her lashes, she asked,

"And what do *you* do?" Nothing in his expression changed, but he looked into her eyes, giving her a terrible sensation of endless falling. After a moment he indicated by a shift of his eyes that she should look under the table. She felt herself blushing scarlet; then, biting her lip, she obeyed. In the darkness below, almost touching her shoes, lay the blade of an axe. Instinctively, before she knew she would do it, she touched her throat. The man smiled, then his eyes once again went out of focus. She put both hands over her heart to calm the pounding, like a fire behind her collarbone.

Vlemk the box-painter opened his eyes a little, raised his eyebrows, and looked at his friends. He looked at the Princess, as if to ask what had happened, then down at his lap. He lifted the sack and began to put the boxes in, one by one. She watched them being taken from her with the anguish of a child losing its treasures. Each horror he moved to the sack was like flesh torn from her, but she kept herself from speaking. When he'd put them all inside and had pulled the pursestring that closed the neck, he pushed back his chair and stood up, nodding to her and gesturing. She too pushed back her chair—breathing shallowly, her legs slightly shaking—and stood up. The poet protested. The man who had the axe raised his head as if in distress, looking at her throat. She tried to look away from him but found herself helpless until the box-painter came around the table and offered her his arm. She seized it and clung tightly. Though she looked back, trailing him to the door, still clinging, no one asked for money. She tried to think about it, but her mind was still full of the image of the axe.

Soon they were on the street, where her driver was waiting, the black and gold carriage gleaming weirdly in the light of the lamps and the distant moon. The driver held the door of the carriage for her, melting into darkness in the way her father had always liked, and Vlemk the box-painter squeezed her arm, more powerfully than he knew—she would have bruises in the morning—then released her and began to back away. Before she knew she would do it, she reached out, sudden as a snake striking, and seized the bag of boxes. He did not seem surprised but only looked at her, expressionless, as if thinking of another way of painting her.

"Let me take it," she said. She could not look at him. "Sell them to me!"

He said nothing, showed nothing, but after a long moment shook his head sadly, a little sternly, and opened his thick, strong fingers so that the bag was hers.

She stepped into the carriage, the door closed behind her, and almost at once she heard the tocking of the horses' hooves and felt the swaying of the carriage.

IO

IT WAS THE BEGINNING of a terrible period for the Princess. Whatever the truth might be, it seemed to her unquestionable that she had glimpsed a world more important than her own, gloomy and malevolent but ferociously alive. In her sleep she would dream of the dark, smoky tavern and see again the tip of the axe peeking out from the skirt of the silent man's coat. Putting on a necklace or walking in a field, she would suddenly find herself not looking at the emeralds or watching the airy pirouette of starlings but gazing, mystified and perhaps a little frightened, at the calm, sleeping face of Vlemk the box-painter, the scum of the earth all around him—the poet who could not write, the violinist who could not play, the grim man who carried an axe and stared at throats.

Strange to say, the boxes, when she laid them out one after another on her table, had no great interest for her now. She looked at them, studied them, but the magic had evaporated. They were pictures, simply— not even very good ones, she occasionally suspected— and though she knew, intellectually, that they were the story of her life or image of her character, she found that something had gone wrong with her: she had no feeling for them. She looked at them each time with

97

renewed disappointment. They might as well have been
sick cartoons. They were not just that, she knew, and
she struggled to feel their significance. Sometimes, indeed, she could feel a frail echo of the original thrill
of alarm—sense herself decaying, know the horror of
death. But when she thought, she knew that the feeling
did not come from the pictures, it came from the tavern,
the silent man's axe. The pictures were boring. It was
because of that, because she had lost all feeling, that
sometimes she sat with the terrible pictures spread out
before her and silently wept.

"Are you all right?" the picture that could talk
would say.

She would sniff, jerk back her head, and nod.

"You certainly are becoming a bore," the picture that
could talk would say. "What ever happened to your
fury?"

" 'Fury,' " the Princess would mock, sniffing. There
it usually ended. But one night when unaccountably the
air smelled of winter, the picture felt cross enough to
press the matter. "That's what I mean," the picture said.
"Why are you so quick to *pounce* on things?"

"The quilt," said the Princess coolly, rising from
her bed.

"Why? That's no fair!" cried the picture. "What did
I say?"

But the Princess had no mercy and put the quilt over
the picture's face.

It was not quite sufficient; she could hear the picture
wailing, like the hum of a mosquito; but she ignored it.

Tiresome as the paintings on the boxes were, or
deeply depressing, not for what they showed but for

the proof they gave her that she was only half alive, a miserable creature displacing air in the world for no good reason — the thought of the tavern filled her with something like the same alarm she had felt when she first stepped through the door. Perhaps that was the answer, it struck her all at once. Immediately she thought of the man with the axe and felt a tingle of fear. Suppose he should indeed kill her! In her mind's eye she saw it vividly, the sudden moving shadow where she had thought there was only a doorway, his rush toward her, coattails flying, the axe uplifted, the man running just a little sideways, coming without a sound. The vision was so clear that it made her cry out, sudden tears filling her eyes. She clenched her fists, then clutched her head, trying to think clearly. Was that perhaps the curse that had fallen on her — a fear of life because she too much feared death? Surely that was wrong! Surely there was nothing in the world that she feared, pain, sickness, madness. . . . Abruptly, reaching her decision almost without knowing it, she rose and snatched up her cloak, crossed to her door, thinking of calling for her carriage driver, then paused, lips pursed, and deciding on another course, threw her cloak across a chair. She quietly opened the door, stepped through, and just as quietly closed it; she looked to left and right, then hurried to the chamber of her maid. When she opened the door without knocking, letting light rush in, the maid sat bolt upright in bed and gave a peeping cry.

"It's all right!" said the Princess.

The maid's eyes widened again, and her small gray mouth fell open.

"I need to borrow some clothes," said the Princess.

And so that night the Princess walked down into the city, alone and in disguise.

Not even the stupidest of the regulars were fooled, but they pretended to be. The Princess stood stiff and erect at the elbow of the ex-violinist. "Do you mind if I sit down?" she asked.

The ex-violinist looked at his friends in befuddlement, then back at the Princess, then violently nodded, reaching out with a jerk of his arm for the chair, to pull it back for her.

It was the strangest, most joyful and terrifying night of her life—as much of it as she could remember. It seemed to her that all she had suspected was true: her ordered life was madness, only this wild, unbridled acceptance of whatever the universe might throw, in its glorious indifference, was true and right. Somehow in her innocent dreams of debauchery she had imagined that she would sing like a gypsy and dance, throw her fists like a man, indulge in unspeakable language. That, when she thought of it now, made her toss back her head and shake violently with laughter. No no, it was nothing like that for the Princess. It was something far more wonderful and grotesque. It was the smell of the armpits of the ex-violinist as he closed her in his arms, almost falling from his chair beside hers in the tavern, raging against music. It was the coldness of the flesh of the sleeping poet when she kissed him on the cheek—she would have sworn he was dead—and the heat in the fingers of the axe-murderer as he slowly lowered his hand onto hers, pinning it to the coarse tavern table, his eyes staring through her.

"Very well," she thought, sometime long after midnight—full of cunning, her eyelids so heavy she had to peek out through the slits, "very well, very well. . . ." She strained futilely to remember what she'd meant to say. The three men's eyes were all glazed and still, like the eyes of dead animals she'd seen beside the road. "Very well," she said again, with conviction, and raised one finger to shake it at the axe-murderer. She made her face ferocious. "I suppose you're aware that my father died?" The murderer looked at her as before. Yes, she thought, yes!, and felt a thrill of aliveness. What was it to artists—a life, a death? She smiled and jerked herself left to look around at the room, pawing abstractly for her glass and straining hard to focus. Smoke, darkness, people, a tall figure, blurred at the edges, standing by the door. She smiled, head lowered, and swung her face back toward the axe-murderer. "*Well*," she said, her voice gone deep. "I imagine you wonder why I'm here!" She laughed, hearing the girlishness, the sweetness. "Ha ha! Ha ha!" She steadied herself, focusing on the murderer's face, and it occurred to her that it was time to speak truthfully. She took a drink from her glass, not looking down from his eyes. "I suppose you're aware that my father died?" she said. "Well!" she said, coming to her senses—she was making a scene; it was absurd. "Very well!" she said, and smiled. The murderer was leaning down, doing something with the axe, under the table. The tall man at the door came toward them and slowly walked past, his arms folded over his chest. He was a policeman. When he was gone, the murderer wiped his forehead. The policeman sat down in the corner of the room. He got out his pipe and stoked it. After a moment, pursing her lips, the Princess said, "I suppose we all die, don't we." She found she was crying.

I I

FOR VLEMK THE BOX-PAINTER, it was not easy to believe his eyes when he found her the next morning, gray as a ghost, one shoe missing, her body in the gutter surrounded by old papers, oyster shells, and frost like bits of glass and white hair. He knew from the instant he first saw her exactly what had happened and all that was wrong with her, for strange to say, she looked, right down to the last detail, like a certain one of the cruel, bitter pictures he'd made of her. He gawked, his knees bent, his arms reaching out, then, clamping down his hat with one hand, ran around her, absurdly looked down for a relatively clean place to plant his knees, shook himself in anger at such foolishness, then dropped down to listen—almost dizzy with dread—for her heartbeat. Was it possible that she'd frozen to death? He heard her heart at once, sound as any drum, and joyfully patted her on the cheek, weeping with relief, then rubbed his hands. "Yes, yes," he exclaimed inside his mind, looking up and down the street, "be quick about it!" Tears ran down his cheeks, cold as ice in the wind. He planted his knees more firmly and thought about where to put his hands to pick her up.

It was only when he was halfway up the hill on his way to the palace, huffing and blowing, the Princess a

103

dead-weight in his arms, that the box-painter's joy at
finding her still alive gave way to worry. What was to
become of her? He'd told himself at first that it was
grief at the death of her father that had brought on this
fling of self-destruction; for indeed, the whole kingdom
had reeled and staggered at the death of the old man. But
now Vlemk was beginning to remember certain things
that disturbed him. He remembered how, when he'd rid-
den in the carriage with her, her gloved hand, laid on his,
had trembled. It had filled him with alarm which he'd
have given more thought to, had he not been, at the
time, too drunk to think of anything but himself. He
remembered, and saw again now, looking down at her
— her head falling limply, slightly turned to one side
as he carried her in his arms — how hollow her cheeks
had looked of late, and how under her eyes she had dark
circles. He thought of the glint he had seen repeatedly
in her eyes when she was angry, a glint that seemed a
little like madness. "Bless me," he said in his mind, and
his distress became greater than before. "How beautiful
she is!" he thought, and did not notice the strangeness
of it, for what he was noticing was quite the opposite,
that she had changed for the worse.

Vlemk's arms and legs were trembling and aching —
"None of us are as young as we used to be," he thought
— and he saw that he must rest before finishing the trek
up the hill. Now that the sun was out, the day had
become quite warm. A maple tree stood beside the road
just ahead of him, and he decided to push that far and
set down his burden for a little underneath it in the
shade. Shortly before he reached the tree, red-gold and
glorious, he saw to his surprise that there was a monk

sitting under it. He felt a touch of dismay, for he had hoped he could get her to the palace without anyone's seeing her; but his weariness was not to be denied. If he carried her much farther he would fall; it was no time for niceties. He entered the sparse shade of the maple with the Princess, bowing politely to the monk as he came in, and lowered her to the grass and fallen leaves on the tree's far side, where the monk might not notice who she was. Vlemk dusted a few bits of dirt from her forehead, straightened her arms and legs — as if arranging her for her funeral, he thought woefully, for in fact she looked astonishingly like the cruel painting he called "The Princess Almost Dead of Despair." Then, wiping away all trace of his tears, Vlemk went around to the side of the tree where the monk was, to keep him occupied.

The monk was an old man as bony and wasted as a person who's lived for years on just air and tea. He sat with the skirts of his cassock hiked up to let the breeze in at his legs — it was a day for picking persimmons or going for one last cool swim in some farmer's pond — and he had his hood thrown back, revealing his large ears and head, as hairless as a darning egg. A stalk of timothy hung down limply from the brown stumps that more or less served him as teeth, and inside his collar, to cut down the scratching, he had burdock leaves.

"Ah! The box-painter!" said the monk, looking up at Vlemk.

Vlemk studied him more closely.

"We met one dark night in a graveyard where I make my home, insofar as I have one," the monk explained.

Vlemk nodded and smiled, remembering now, though only dimly. He also remembered that when he'd last seen the monk the curse of the picture had not yet been put on him. By gestures and winces, he revealed his new condition.

The monk smiled and nodded, utterly unperturbed. "That's the world, my friend," he said. "Sin . . ."— he looked up into the tree as if the notion pleased him— "Sin is all around us. The whole of creation is one vast sin." He smiled.

Vlemk scowled to show that he was not in agreement, or that at any rate he did not consider his curse to be a punishment for his sins but, on the contrary, a stroke of blind chance.

"Matter itself is sin," said the monk. "This is a hard lesson, my child"—he reached toward Vlemk to pat his foot with one skeletal hand. Not instinctively, but to show how he felt, Vlemk drew his foot back. The monk closed his eyes and smiled as benignly as before. "I know, I know. You don't believe me. No one does. Nevertheless it's the case, I believe. I'm an old, old man, as you can see by these teeth—close to the grave, beyond all desire to make up stories. I can give you my assurance as a Christian ascetic, I was never so happy in all my days as I've been since the night I accepted the proposition that all matter, all earthly physicality, is filth and corruption."

Vlemk sighed irritably, reached down for a stick on the grass beside him, and considered whether he was strong enough to continue on his way up to the palace. His legs were still weak, the strength in his fingers so diminished that he could barely break the stick with two hands. "Very well, I'll sit here a moment longer," he thought. Much as he disliked the monk's opinions,

Vlemk joked to himself a little bitterly, the monk did no more harm in the world than, say, an axe-murderer, and Vlemk had tolerated that, though perhaps not with pleasure.

"Ah yes, ah yes," the monk said, nodding. "I understand the pull! That lovely lady there—" He gestured toward the Princess lying still as a corpse on the far side of the tree. Carefully, or so it seemed to Vlemk, the monk avoided looking at her. "Physicality has its beauties, but they're devil-lures and delusions. Take my word for it. Everything passes. That's the one great truth, this side of Heaven." He glanced at Vlemk, oddly shy. "Symbols, that's their value," he said. "Signs of what might be. This timothy stalk—" He pointed at the stalk he chewed on even as he lectured. "All the juice has been gone out of it for months now. That's why I chew on it."

As he spoke, a bee, for some reason not flying but buzzing in the grass, struggling along through it, found purchase on his ankle and, still buzzing, beating its small wings with the fury of a damned soul in fire, climbed up on top of his foot and settled, gradually calming itself, between the monk's first and second toes. Vlemk leaned forward slowly, not to alarm the bee, and pointed, imagining that the monk had not noticed it was there.

"Let him rest," said the monk. "He has his troubles too." He shook his head sadly. "A tiny soul trapped in the horror of materiality—sick unto death, it may well be; certainly it *will* be, sooner or later. For him, all the pain in the world is right there in that small body." He pointed at the bee.

"You're not afraid he'll sting you?" asked Vlemk with gestures.

Ever so slightly, the monk shrugged. "Let him sting me. Not that he will, I think. But suppose he does? Who am I to complain? Up there where we can't see them, blinded by daylight"—he pointed up into the tree, or through it—"stars are exploding. Have you ever seen an elephant die?" He rolled his eyes up, then closed them, shaking his head.

Rested, the bee began beating its wings again, and apparently whatever had been wrong before was no longer wrong, for it lifted from its place between the monk's two toes, flying backward, then forward, or so it seemed to Vlemk, and zoomed toward the trunk of the tree. It moved on past the trunk in the direction of the Princess, and suddenly Vlemk's heart floundered. It flew straight to the Princess's lower lip and settled there. Vlemk was up at once, leaping like a flea, and dropped down on his knees beside the Princess and flailed his right hand above her face to drive the bee off. Horrified, too shocked to flail his hand again, he saw the bee lower its stinger into the pink of her lip—slowly, deliberately, it seemed to Vlemk—then fly away. The Princess's eyes popped open and she gave a little cry. She raised her hand to her mouth.

"Oh no!" Vlemk exclaimed without a sound.

"He'll die now," the monk said. "You've killed him; or he's killed himself." He still had his eyes closed. "That's what comes of falling in love with the things of this world. Let them be—let them batter and claw themselves to death, as they will. In the end they'll be better off for it, believe me. Freed souls, pure spirit! The

same as they were before matter undid them, with all
its serpentine twists and accidents." The monk waved
his hand, still with his eyes closed. "I know, I know,"
he said wearily, "You don't believe me."

The Princess rolled her eyes to left and right in panic,
poking at her lip with two fingers, trying to make out
what had happened and where she was.

"It's all right," said Vlemk with gestures. "A bee
stung you."

She stared at him, closed her eyes again, then opened
them and touched her mouth with the tip of just one
finger.

The monk stretched out on his back, as if dismissing
them.

Gingerly, as if her body was as bruised as her dress
was torn, the Princess sat up and looked up the hill
toward the palace. "What am I doing here?" she asked.
Then her eyes widened and she raised her hand to keep
him from answering.

Rising, giving a little bow, Vlemk invited her to continue with him if she was ready. She seemed to consider
it carefully, then at last nodded.

Until they reached the palace gate, the Princess walking with both hands on Vlemk's arm, putting her feet
down one after another with the care of an invalid,
occasionally reaching up with a troubled gesture, pushing her hair back or briefly covering her eyes, neither
Vlemk nor the Princess said a word. At the gate she
hesitated, looking in toward the great, arched door like
a stranger, then glanced at Vlemk and, after an instant,
bowed her head. With her right foot she abstractly drew
something in the yellow-white pebbles of the road, a

small, perfect square like the beginning of one of his boxes. "Will you come in with me?" she asked.

Vlemk sighed, imagining what the servants would say behind their hands, what they would suppose about his bringing her home in this bedraggled condition, long after breakfast time, her lower lip bright red and swollen. She was looking at him earnestly, on the verge of withdrawing her question, and, to save her that further embarrassment, however trifling, Vlemk the box-painter nodded and gave a little shrug.

Now they had another problem. It seemed that the Princess had no key to the gate—if she'd started out with one, she'd lost it somewhere—and so they took two stones from the side of the road and banged on the iron, at first politely, then with all their force. Suddenly the door of the palace opened and the Princess's greyhounds came bounding out, followed by a stooped old man. Barking noisily, leaping like deer, the dogs charged the gate as if trained to eat intruders alive. There were five of them, lean as eels, their eyes rolling wildly and their teeth like razors, hurling spittle to left and right. "Smakkr! Lokkr! Zmölr!" cried the Princess, but even at the sound of her voice they seemed not to know her, bounding up again and again and biting empty air. She put her hand between the bars of the gate, then snatched it back. "Down, Klauz!" she shouted, furious. "Eerzr! Down boy!" The old man was still some distance back, moving without hurry, leaning hard on his cane, throwing a shout to the dogs from time to time, but only from a feeble civility. Now, however, the most cunning of the dogs, or perhaps the most suspicious, was showing signs of confusion. He hung back, head tipped, still barking as ferociously as the others but no longer bounding up. The Princess, too, had noticed it. "Zmölr!" she cried, as loud as she could shout, her face red with anger, and now another dog, perking up his ears, showed uncertainty. Suddenly the two dogs were snarling at the others, interfering with their leaps, and in an instant all five dogs had changed their ways completely, whimpering and whistling in their throats like puppies, pressing their narrow noses between the bars, crying for a pat from the Princess. The old man, seeing it, began to hurry.

"Fool!" shouted the Princess when he was near enough to hear, "is this how you manage our watchdogs?"

"Oh Mistress, Mistress," cried the gatekeeper, tears running down his face, and wrung his hands.

"Look at me!" said the Princess, as if her filthy, torn clothes were the fault of the gatekeeper and his dogs. "Look at me!" she raged, bursting into tears. "You'll pay for this, villain! As sure as I'm standing here you'll pay for this!"

"Oh Mistress, Mistress," he wailed again, as if it were the only phrase he knew, wringing his hands more fervently than before.

"Undo the gate, you stupid old man!" the Princess shouted. "Must we just *stand* here?" Timidly, Vlemk touched her arm to calm her. She pretended not to notice.

Nearly falling in his haste, the old man got out his key ring, turned the lock, and began pushing at the gate. The five dogs leaped all around him, joyfully yapping.

"Fool," said the Princess, seizing the gatebars in her own two hands, her eyes filled with tears, "can you do *nothing* right?"

That instant, with her hair flying out around her head, crackling with the lightening-bolt charge of her anger, the Princess looked exactly like the picture Vlemk had called "The Princess Gives Way to Wrath." Her cheeks were so bright that Vlemk held his breath.

Almost at once his senses came back to him. He rubbed his hands on the sides of his trousers and stared morosely at the ground. He understood well enough that it was the Princess's fright and feeling of having been betrayed when her dogs turned against her, also her shame at coming home in this condition, looking like a strumpet who'd been run over by a cart, conceivably also a touch of embarrassment over the fact that Vlemk had been witness to it all, had seen with his own eyes how the palace, so well-run and orderly even at the height of her father's illness was now reduced to chaos, when the rule was hers. Even so, her anger seemed excessive, in fact mad, as was the fear he'd seen in her when they'd first arrived here, her desire that he come in with her and protect her from the glances of her servants. He shook his head, hardly knowing he was doing it.

Now, since the gate stood wide open, they went in. She was hardly less fierce with the servants inside. Vlemk moved away from her while she yelled at them, and occupied himself with the paintings on the walls, family portraits. He saw how the king had looked once, or anyway, how the painter had chosen to see him, tall and elegant but very stern. His hand around the ball of his cane was, for no clear reason, clenched, as if in a moment he might raise it and brandish it, and his hat was cocked forward, not jauntily but somehow fiercely, as if it were intended to cushion the blow if he should suddenly choose to butt someone. Her mother, on the other hand, was the soul of sweetness and gentleness, such gentleness that it verged on feebleness. One wouldn't have been surprised to learn (and indeed it was true) that she'd been dead for years and years.

The Princess's chambermaid came running past him, her hands over her face, weeping.

"A terrible business," thought Vlemk, and shook his head. The Princess's hands, he saw, were jerking and twitching. It was terrible! A tragedy! But what was he to do?

Now servants were running in every direction, weeping and wringing their hands or tearing out their hair. When the Princess had finished with the last of them, she came to him and said, "Wretches! I have half a mind to order them all whipped!"

Vlemk said nothing but stared at the floor with his head bowed.

"Would you care for tea?" asked the Princess.

"Perhaps another time," Vlemk said in gestures, "You should rest."

Quickly, before she could think better of it, she reached out to touch his arm with her trembling hand. "Must you leave so soon?" she asked. "Just *one* cup of tea?"

Vlemk shook his head, then shrugged and nodded.

"Tea!" shouted the Princess, as if expecting the paintings to jump down off the walls in fearful obedience and serve it. Then more quietly she said, "This way," and led him towards another room. Strange to say, eager as she was to have him stay longer with her, she said not a word to him as she led him to the door, opened it and, not quite meeting his eyes, waved him in. Just inside the door Vlemk stopped short and wiped his hands on his trousers, utterly at a loss. Though it was true that there were chairs and tables in the room, it was also true that the room was the Princess's bedroom; and Vlemk was becoming more and more, these days, a man of rule and decorum. Perhaps it was the influence of the middle-class visitors who were of late his main customers, or perhaps it was the influence of the mellower paintings themselves — or again, conceivably, it was the queer muttering that for a moment he imagined to be coming from the sinister paintings he'd made on the boxes, indifferently scattered around the room. But whatever the reason, Vlemk the box-painter felt wretchedly out of place there where she slept and did all that is most private, and if he dared, he would have fled like a rabbit. But too late to worry about it now, he saw; for that minute a serving girl arrived, sniffing and hiding her face, bringing the tea-tray.

"Over on the table," said the Princess. When the tea things were in place the Princess sent the serving girl out again and invited Vlemk to take a chair. No sooner had he come where she could see him than the picture that could talk cried out, "Vlemk! Vlemk!"

Vlemk smiled and threw up his hands as joyfully as an old man when he sees his son. "My little masterpiece," he cried in gesture, and in his delight did not even remember that she was the reason he could never speak aloud.

"Oh, Vlemk," cried the picture, "take me home, I beg you! She's so cruel I'd die of sorrow if you'd made me of anything less durable than paint!"

The Princess became still with rage, more angry even than he'd imagined her in his painting. She was so angry all the breath went out of her, and her face became as gray as old snow. "Do take her back by all means!" she said as soon as she could speak. "All she does is whine and revile me and complain! Take her back at once and good riddance!"

"I can't do that," said Vlemk in gesture. "She's your own very self, a picture so real it can speak. Surely you can find a way to live with your own very self!"

But the Princess was too angry to be reasoned with, slamming the table with the flat of her hand so that the box made little jumps up and down. "Get it away from me! Take it back! Get it from my sight!" cried the Princess.

"Very well," said Vlemk with gestures, humbly; and then he began to nod up and down like an old philosopher, for an idea was taking shape in his mind. "Perhaps," he said in gesture, "I can change the picture's personality a little, so that when you look at it again you may find it somewhat more acceptable."

"Change it to a spider, for all I care," said the Princess. "Just get it *out* of here, away from my sight!"

"I *like* my personality," said the picture.

"*Will* you shut up?" screamed the Princess, and raised both fists above her head to smash it. But Vlemk was too quick for her, and soon the box was in his pocket and his feet were on the road again, trudging toward the city.

12

VLEMK THE BOX-PAINTER thought long and hard about the idea that had come to him in the Princess's room. Sometimes he thought the idea was stark mad, so that he would clutch his head, eyes wide open, and whisper "Woe is me! What's become of me?" At other times he thought it magnanimous beyond the wildest dreams of any ordinary mortal, and he would put on such airs that to everyone he met he seemed insufferable. But usually he hung undecided between opinions and could do nothing but pull at his knuckles and rock back and forth on his stool, with his eyes tight shut and his lips between his teeth, like a woman who has a baby that won't stop crying. The idea that had come to him in the Princess's room was this: that perhaps he could alter the painting here and there, removing those hints of imperfection in its character, so that it was no longer a true-to-life miniature of the Princess but a picture of what she might be if she had no faults at all. Then she would surely like it, he thought—how could she not?, especially, considering the fact that (but ah, this was the hard part!) it would no longer talk back to her; indeed, since it would no longer be a perfect imitation, it would no longer talk at all. There would go not only the picture's chief glory, the unanswerable proof that no one

116

in the world had ever captured such a likeness in a painting on a box — no small matter, to Vlemk, for he had hardly gotten where he was without a trace of artistic vanity — but also, alas, Vlemk's hopes of regaining his speech, since it was the picture that had put the curse on him, and the picture — the picture or no one! — that must take it off.

The idea of living out his life as a mute was by no means a pleasant one to Vlemk, for though it is true that he'd been mute for some time and had in a way gotten used to it, indeed, had learned secrets about everyone around him, thanks to his affliction, that had enriched his knowledge of the world immeasurably, with no small effect on his box-painting, it is also true that, with the optimism natural to living creatures, however they may resist it or in their worst moods mock it, the box-painter had always gone on hoping in secret that his bad luck would someday change to good and the picture would relent. Now, sitting in his busy studio with the picture that could talk on the table before him, his apprentices sawing, hammering and painting, or sweeping up the sawdust, cleaning brushes, and talking with visitors — the tiny image of the Princess chattering happily, telling him of life at the palace, how the King had died, how the Princess had frequently covered her with a quilt — Vlemk wrung his hands and rocked back and forth and again and again considered the idea that had come to him. He was so abstracted that he hardly looked up when people spoke to him, and so sick with indecision — whether to do this or, on the other hand, do that — that he would sometimes heave such a deep sigh of woe that people would step back from him in fear.

"If I'm really going to do it," he told himself, "I should get out my brushes and start painting." But day after day he did nothing but sit rocking and sighing, weighing the arguments on this side and that. He thought of the picture he'd painted of the barmaid and how it had seemingly changed her life. On the other hand he thought of the incident with the bee, how in his attempt to be helpful he'd done nothing but harm. Though the monk's opinions might offend and annoy him, he couldn't help but see that there was truth in them: what good was it, loving this physical world—gardens and Princesses, barmaids and poor trembling maniacs? Where would they be in a thousand years? Painting them was one thing—a record for posterity—but throwing away all one's hopes for their sake. . . . "No, no!" thought Vlemk, "absurd!" Also, there was the matter of the feelings of the picture herself. Had he really any right to deprive his creation of speech? Is all life not sacred? Is not the true work of art a thing greater than its maker? Indeed, wasn't it the case that a work of art, once out of the artist's hands—if not before—belonged to no one, or to all humanity? He began to find it hard to meet the eyes of the picture on the box. He could see that she was worried and suspicious, watching him like a hawk. "How queer it is," he thought, "that what ought to be the noblest, most selfless act of my life should be made to seem sordid and inhumane!" Vlemk clenched his fists. He should have known, of course, from the moment the picture first opened its mouth. She was unnatural, a piece of Devil's work! Indeed, had she not ensorcelled him? And hadn't she clung to her meanness through good times and bad times, chattering endlessly, refusing to let Vlemk get out a word? Well, her days of meanness were ended, thought Vlemk with a terrible scowl.

But no sooner would Vlemk reach this sensible decision than the picture would speak up and charm him again with that seeming childlike innocence, and he would feel she was breaking his heart. The terrible truth was that he loved with all his heart that saucy, incorrigible litle picture on the box—and no doubt also the Princess, since the two were identical; but *that* he would not think about. However fine the reason, and even though she stubbornly held out on him, refusing to lift the curse, he would rather be dead than change a line on that complicated face.

"Vlemk?" the picture would say, smiling to hide her fear, "A penny for your thoughts?"

Vlemk would shrug guiltily and would realize that among the many other thoughts was this one, shameful as it might be: that if he played his cards right—since the picture was so happy to be home again—he could get her to cancel the curse of silence and *then* perhaps repaint her. At once, at the thought of such treachery, he would become glum—irritable and irritating so that the picture would look baffled and hurt, then gradually become crochety, and in the end fall silent. This went on for days and days, and he seemed no nearer a decision than he'd been in the beginning.

One night when his anger at himself was intense, Vlemk stood up abruptly and put on his hat and coat and went down to the tavern. All the regulars were there as usual, the barmaid smiling and showing her ring, for she was newly engaged to be married. The axe-murderer, the ex-poet, and the ex-musician were seated together in their usual corner, glaring out at everyone like weasels in a henhouse. Vlemk the box-painter stood pondering with his thumbs in his suspenders, then at last went over to them. As he seated himself he signalled to the barmaid, and said in gestures, when she came to him, "Wine, my dear—the best in the house! I'm paying myself, since now my boxes are selling well, and I can't accept your charity any longer." When he was sure she'd understood all this and when he'd dismissed her protests that indeed she must pay, she owed it to him, he added, "Also, the best wine you have in the house for my three old friends."

The barmaid said, "But they already have our best wine—more than they can drink and God knows far more than they deserve. Look!"

Vlemk turned to look and, sure enough, in front of each of them stood a costly bottle of wine not yet half empty. "Well, well," he said to himself, then glanced at the barmaid and shrugged and signalled for wine for just himself. When he turned to his friends again and asked in gestures what accounted for this good fortune, they looked at one another with malevolent grins, trembling like leaves in a strong breeze, until at last the poet said, "You don't fool us, pretending you don't know, you sly old fox! But if you think we're ashamed to say it, you're quite mistaken! We too can debauch our art and make it fill our poor stomachs."

Vlemk looked from one to another of them, wounded, then opened his hands as a sign that he failed to understand.

"Ah," said the ex-poet to the ex-violinist, "how he

loves to mock, this ex-box-painter!" His cheek muscles twitched and a vein stood out in his temple. The ex-violinist laughed harshly and, from behind his spectacles, threw a wink at the axe-murderer.

The ex-poet pointed one finger at Vlemk, the finger only inches from Vlemk's nose. "You," he said, "paint foolish pretty pictures, exactly what your idiot customers would paint for themselves, if they had wit enough. You're right, of course. Why should men of genius go hungry while stupid little insects eat potatoes and gravy?" He winked at the ex-violinist, who winked at the murderer. The ex-poet pushed his flaxen haired face close to Vlemk's, as if daring him to scoff. "I write verses for a cardboard container corporation: 'Got troubles? Outfox 'em! Box em!' "

"I write music," said the ex-violinist. "I take themes from famous symphonies. Soon every time you hear the work of a famous composer, you'll think 'Cardboard boxes!' "

Vlemk looked sadly at the murderer.

The murderer smiled. "I chop up wooden boxes to make the phosphor sticks people buy in those little cardboard boxes. They're getting to be all the rage, these phosphor sticks. They're easier than a flint. Also, sometimes children burn down hotels with them. Ha ha!"

Vlemk was so depressed at the thought of the murderer's chopping up wooden boxes that when his wine came he could hardly raise his glass. It was as if an enormous weight of snow lay over him. "So this is what everything comes down to in the end," he thought, staring at the dirt in the fingernails of the two fingers closed on his wine glass stem. "All our early promise, all our grand ideals!"

Though he felt a little cross, or worse than cross, as if his heart had turned to ice—useless to deny it—it was no good berating his fellow artists. Hunger and poverty are powerful persuaders, and so was the policeman who'd taken to sitting in the tavern nights, smoking his pipe and occasionally glancing at the murderer. Nor could Vlemk deny that he himself had unwittingly contributed to their decline. In his cynical period, he had spoken with pleasure and excitement of his work on the "Reality boxes"—his malevolent pictures of the Princess. In his mellower period he'd had nothing to say. Indeed, he had nothing to say even now. It was just one more instance, he told himself, of spirit weighed down by matter until it no longer knows itself. He sighed.

"Very well," thought Vlemk, and leaned forward slowly, bidding his friends good-evening and putting the cork in the bottle, the bottle in his pocket, then walking up the street to his house and up the stairs to his studio, where he opened up his paints.

"What are you doing?" cried the picture as she saw the brush approaching.

He tried to say in gestures, "I'm hoping to make you even finer than you are," but the picture on the box was in such a wild panic, her little bosom heaving, her eyes opened wide, that in the end he only smiled as reassuringly as possible, sucked in his lower lip between his teeth, and began to paint. He painted for a week without stopping, and when he finished, the painting looked—to Vlemk, at least—exactly like the Princess except with none of her faults. Nearly everyone who looked at it said it was the most beautiful, most angelic face in the world, so true to life—or at least to some barely imaginable possibility — that you could literally hear it breathing. But the picture no longer talked. Not everyone was persuaded, of course, about the picture's perfection. When he showed it to his apprentices they frowned and looked evasive, and at last the fat one said, "It looks sort of the same as before."

Vlemk gestured wildly, as if to say, "I paint for a week — me! Vlemk! — and the painting looks the same as before?"

The fat one ducked his head. "I just said *sort* of," he explained.

Little did they know, he thought sorrowfully. Though it watched him as if in a jury, the picture had become, like himself, as mute as a stone.

13

COWARDLY OR NOT, he could not bear to take the picture up himself—and no reason he should, he convinced himself; there was no reason the Princess should have anything to say to him. Nevertheless he was secretly puzzled, for a week after sending the re-painted picture by the youngest of his apprentices, Vlemk had still heard nothing. Then a message arrived, brought to him in person by the driver with the top hat and the polished boots. It was a small, white card on which the Princess had written, in a feeble hand, an urgent invitation to the palace.

Vlemk frowned and studied the face of the driver for some sign. Behind the driver's head there were low, leaden clouds. The driver showed nothing, standing with his hands folded, gazing solemnly—almost tragically, Vlemk would have said—at the floor. In haste, the box-painter hung up his frock, put on his good black Sunday coat, gave instructions to his apprentices on the business of the day, and went to the carriage with the driver.

At the top of the hill, the gates to the palace were open wide, and the dogs lay still beside the road, as if someone had put a spell on them. The gatekeeper made no move to interfere with the entrance of the carriage but stood back, with his hat off, crying out as Vlemk peeked through the window, "God be with you, sir!" Vlemk frowned more deeply.

At the high arched door the carriage stopped abruptly and the driver jumped down from his seat in front so quickly, for all his dignity, that the door was opened for Vlemk before the carriage had stopped swaying. The driver's face, as he took Vlemk's arm to help him down, was so abysmally solemn that Vlemk for an instant hesitated, narrowing his eyes and pushing his bearded face close to the driver's for a better look; but the man's expression told him nothing, and so, with an increasing sense of urgency, Vlemk went up the steps into the palace.

Nothing was at all as it had been before. In fact, so transformed was the palace when he entered that he stopped in his tracks and snatched his hat off in order to think more clearly. First, all the walls had been washed till they shone like new-cut marble, and everywhere he looked there were new, fresh flowers — rising stalks and blooms, shimmering and blazing, ferns and white ribbons, climbing in such profusion toward the skylight overhead that one might have thought one had shrunk to the size of a ladybug and were standing at the bottom of a florist's box. Second, and more ominous, the servants moved back and forth as quietly as swallows, or stood in doorways, no more talkative than owls. No one anywhere was smiling even slightly, not even the chief butler's grandchildren over by the fountain. "This is bad," thought Vlemk, standing with his shoulders hunched, rubbing his palms together, squinting and pursing his lips.

Then suddenly the door to the Princess's room opened, and, to Vlemk's amazement, out rushed the Prince with the moustache.

"You!" cried the Prince, with an expression so twisted and uncertain one couldn't tell whether it was rage or the hope that, now that Vlemk was here, all might at last be well.

Vlemk bowed and nodded, then tipped his head inquiringly.

"Come quickly," said the Prince, "she's been asking for you since she wakened." Even now his expression was neither one thing or another but filled with contradictions. He seized Vlemk's arm, but Vlemk stood rooted, still with his head tipped, his hands opened out like a beggar's. At last the Prince understood. "You haven't heard?" he asked. When Vlemk went on waiting, the Prince explained. "The Princess is ill! No one has the faintest idea what the trouble is. I came over from my neighboring kingdom as soon as I heard." His face became more stern and his grip on the handle of his ornamented cane somewhat frightened. "I refuse to let it happen! Believe me, I'll move heaven and earth, if I have to. . . ." Sweat had popped out on his forehead, and he took a swipe at it with his sleeve, then lowered his head and frowned like a goat.

At the news that the Princess was seriously ill, Vlemk's knees turned to rubber, and to keep himself from falling he had to cling to the Prince with both hands.

"In my personal opinion, it's the picture you did of her," said the Prince, and his hand closed still more tightly on the cane. Anger lit his eyes, but then the next instant his expression was full of doubt, panicky. "Then again, perhaps everything's just the opposite of what it seems," he said, and quickly looked away. His gaze went running around the room. As if in hopes that Vlemk might resolve his confusion, he tugged abruptly and rather sternly at Vlemk's arm, moving him in the direction of the door, and Vlemk, after a moment's resistance, gave up and followed.

The moment the Prince and the box-painter entered, the servants and doctors who were gathered around the Princess's four-poster bed drew back the curtains and slipped out of the way like shadows. In this room too there were flowers everywhere, especially around the bed. The Princess's head lay as white on its pillow as a pearl in its crimson casque, her arms above the covers, and in her white, white hands, she held the box with the picture Vlemk had altered. As if he didn't mean to but couldn't help himself, the Prince pushed past Vlemk and went up to her first, bent quickly, impulsively, to kiss her on the forehead, then turned away, blushing, signalling for Vlemk to come and help. As soon as he thought Vlemk could not see him, the Prince covered his face with his hands like a man stifling a groan and turned his back.

Somewhat timidly, Vlemk approached near enough to touch her pale cheek. Then he stood looking down at her, drawing his hand back to the other hand, with which he was holding his hat. After a moment, with a feeble flutter, the Princess opened her eyes.

"Vlemk," she said softly, with infinite sadness and more affection than she'd ever before shown him.

Instantly, Vlemk's eyes swam with tears. He nodded,

sniffled, and bent forward a little to show that he'd heard.

When she tried to speak again, it seemed that she was too feeble to bring a sound out; but after a moment she managed to say, "Thank you for coming. I was terrified that I might die without seeing you, to put your heart at rest."

Vlemk, hearing these words, opened his eyes wide to stare at her. "Nonsense," he exclaimed, and then, seeing that she seemed not even to notice that he'd spoken, he seized both her hands.

Angrily, the Prince pushed in beside the painter. "You're not going to die!" he cried, his eyes bright as glass. He turned to look with all his fury at Vlemk. All Vlemk could make out was a blur of pinkish light. Turning to the Princess again, the Prince cried out, "You're getting *better* my dear girl!" To the Princess his guilty concern was touching and amusing, though she was careful to hide what she felt.

"No no, dear Prince," she said and sighed, looking at the Prince's trembling face. His teeth were grinding and tears were now streaming down his bright pink cheeks —tears of love for her, she knew, such innocent, open-hearted love—though also, she knew he was hiding something—that it seemed to her criminal that she should trouble him so, be so unworthy of his goodness. Not that she was any longer filled with self-hatred. What more atonement could anyone ask of her than the atonement she was making, death for her sins and crimes? Yet how they had stooped and clasped their hands like supplicants! She did like that, no use denying it! The feeling of queenliness it gave her tempted her for a moment to say no more to either of them, to spare them further pain; but then a kind of heaviness came over her—almost, she thought, like a feeling of old age, or at any rate righteousness—and she felt that, quite simply, she didn't have it in her to die without leaving things straight and clear, clean and open as sunlight, let them handle it as they would. For die she must; her heart was set on it.

Vlemk the box-painter stood pulling first at his left hand, then at his right, filled with alarm at the Princess's words "put your heart at rest." It was just as he feared, he saw. It was he who had brought her to this sorry pass; and she, knowing that sooner or later he must see what he had done, was eager, for his sake, to deny him any guilt, rise above all such pettiness to deathly, sweet wisdom. She was smiling like an old mother cat. Anxiously Vlemk looked from the face of the Princess to the tear-stained, indignant red face of the Prince. But though he wracked his brains, Vlemk could think of no way of preventing her from doing what she intended. Her labor so far had greatly drained her, he saw. Her hands had fallen away from the box she'd been holding, leaving it resting on the covers on her waist.

"Vlemk," said the Princess, her voice growing feebler and feebler, "I was wrong when I told you the original picture on the box was not a good likeness. When I saw the new picture, after you'd made it perfect, I saw with terrible certainty how far I was from the person I imagined myself, how surely I was becoming, from moment to moment, more like those other things you painted."

"New picture?" said the Prince.

The Princess continued, ignoring him, "Seeing the

disparity between what I am and what I wish to be I have come to the only happiness possible for such a wretch as I am, the sad joy of the old philosophers who at least 'knew themselves.' " She lowered her pale blue eyelids and tears slipped warmly from her eyes, "That," she continued, when her voice was in control again, " — that is why I can no longer go on living and have purposely declined to this pitiful state. I want you not to feel guilty when I am dead, just as I hope my dear friend the Prince — "

Here the Princess was dramatically interrupted. Neither she nor Vlemk had noticed that at her mention of the talking picture on the box, the Prince had widened his eyes in horror, everything slowly coming clear to him, and in the first wild impulse of his recognition he had snatched the box from where it lay on the covers and had run to throw it into the fire in the fireplace. There he remained, looking sterner and more guilty than ever. Now it seemed to the Princess — and it was partly because of this that her sentence had broken off — that she was, she herself, on fire all over; and the same instant there came a wail of pain and terror from the fireplace — "Vlemk! Tell her it's not my fault! Oh Master, dear Master, *save* me!"

At the cry of the painting, the curse was lifted, and Vlemk, running toward the picture, cried out over his shoulder in a loud voice, "You're mistaken, Princess! Spare the picture and spare yourself!" The words rang as loudly as thunder in the room. "She's not an impossible ideal, she's your own very self! Otherwise how could she speak?"

The Prince heard none of this, for the instant the cry

came from the fireplace he whirled around without
thinking — Vlemk was still three or four paces away —
to snatch out the box and sprinkle it with water and
save the poor picture's life.

"Is it possible?" cried the Princess, flushing with
pleasure and embarrassment, "is it possible that I have
become exactly like the picture on the box?"

"Vlemk," cried the picture, coughing a little and
blinking soot from her eyes, "I hope you don't think—"

Suddenly understanding, Vlemk hit his forehead with
the palm of his hand, so hard he nearly knocked himself
over. "Treachery!" he bellowed. "You could talk all
the time!"

"I could?" asked the picture in seeming amazement,
and shot a glance at Vlemk and the Princess to see how
much trouble she was in. "You won't believe it," the
picture said, "but—"

"No we certainly won't!" snapped the Princess.
Though she'd been pale as a ghost just a moment ago,
she was suddenly as healthy and lively as could be.
"Shameless little vixen!" the Princess exclaimed, "you
pretended you couldn't talk, just to spite poor Vlemk,
and you wouldn't let *him* talk, miserable as he was, until
your life depended on it! What a horrible, horrible little
creature!"

"Horrible?" cried the picture, bursting into tears.
"We're in this together, remember! If I can talk, it's
because I'm exactly like you! So who's the horrible little
creature?"

The Princess blanched and drew her hand to her
bosom. Her face went red with anger, then white. When
it had struck with full force, she was so shocked by the

revelation that her eyes rolled up almost out of sight.

The Prince was anxiously pulling at his moustache, waving his cane with his left hand, trying to understand. "Now wait," he said. "If I rightly follow this ridiculous business, you"—he pointed to Vlemk, squinting—"you changed the picture to get rid of the little imperfections, is that right?"

"Exactly," said Vlemk, then looked confused. "At least I thought I did."

The Prince's look became thoughtful. "If it had worked, and if the Princess had failed to come up to the standard of the picture, you'd have been mute for the rest of your life!"

The Princess and the picture looked at Vlemk, then away, embarrassed.

"If it had worked, yes," said Vlemk, frowning and scratching his head. "But somehow the picture was able to outwit me and hang onto her powers. It's a mystery."

The picture looked pleased with herself, and privately, the Princess was smiling a little too.

"Is it really such a mystery?" asked the Prince with a laugh. Suddenly he was enjoying himself, as if some burden had been miraculously lifted. There was no longer any trace of the mingled anxiety and anger. He was standing much taller, no longer gripping his cane like a weapon but playing with it, balancing it on the tip of one finger while he talked. "Surely," he said, "surely my dear Vlemk, you painted what you *thought* was a picture of perfection, but it came out exactly as it had been before you started!"

"That must be it," said Vlemk, eyes widening, and he nodded. He glanced at the Princess, then over at the box, and to his surprise saw that both of them were crying. "What's this?" he said, "did I say something wrong?"

"You loved me!" said the Princess and the box, both at once. "How *could* you?" Neither of them could say another word, because both of them were sobbing.

Vlemk, confounded, looked over at the Prince for help.

The Prince shrugged broadly, grinning. "God help you, Vlemk. For most men *one* such unpredictable creature would be enough!" He gave the cane a little toss, so that it went gracefully end over end and came down onto his fingertip, where he balanced it as before. "Well," he said, "since everything seems to be all right again, I'd better hurry home to my wife." He turned to leave.

"*Wife!*" shrieked the Princess and the picture at once.

The Prince's face reddened and the cane fell off balance. He grabbed it. "How was I to tell you?" he said. "You were sick—perhaps dying, for all I knew. . . ."

"You're married?" asked Vlemk.

"Two weeks ago," said the Prince. "Politics, you see. But when I heard that the Princess—"

"You did the right thing," said Vlemk at once. Abruptly, he laughed. "I *thought* you were acting a little strangely!"

Neither the picture or the Princess even smiled. "Oh yes," said the Princess and angrily rolled her head from side to side. "*You* can laugh. What if I'd gotten better because I thought he loved me and then I'd found out? Say what you like, it's a cruel, cruel world full of falsehood and trickery and delusions!"

"It's true, all too true," said Vlemk, trying not to smile. "All the same, I notice there's color in your cheeks. One way or another it seems we have muddled through!"

In secret, the Princess was noticing the same thing. As a matter of fact she had a feeling that if she put her mind to it, she could jump up out of bed and dance. Nothing could please her more than having the Prince with the moustache as only a good friend—he was a wonderful horseman—and not have to worry about that other business. The difficulty was that any minute now he would leave, and so would Vlemk, and there were important matters not yet decided between Vlemk and herself. The thought of his leaving was like a knife in her heart, she would gladly give up her life, her very bones and flesh, and be nothing but a summary warmth around him, a patch of sunlight on his head, anything at all, but near him. Yet try as she might, she could think of no way to keep him here now except petulance and sulking.

"Well," Vlemk was saying now, fiddling with his hat, stealing a glance at the flowers near the door.

"Oh yes," said the Princess bitterly, "trickery and delusion are just fine with you. They're the stock and trade of an artist."

Vlemk looked at her, then down at his shoes, and sighed.

Her eyes became cunning. It crossed her mind that if she knew how to put some kind of curse on him, he'd figure out some way to be near her till the day she lifted it, which would be never.

"Well, it's getting late," the Prince said.

Vlemk the box-painter nodded.

All the while the box had been watching them all with her lips slightly pursed. Suddenly she said, "Vlemk, why don't you marry the Princess and come live with us?"

"Yes why not?" said the Princess quickly, a little crazily. She felt her face stinging, an enormous blush rushing into her cheeks.

"Me?" Vlemk said, then hastily added, "I was thinking the same thing myself!"

"Wonderful!" cried the Prince. "We can visit each other and go riding!"

Vlemk smiled eagerly. The thought of riding a horse made him faint with terror.

"You mean we—you and I—" stammered the Princess. Her face went pale green, then red, then white.

"If you like," Vlemk said.

"Oh Vlemk, Vlemk, I'm sorry about the curse!" the picture wailed. "It was just—I mean. . . ." Now all at once her words came tumbling. "One has to have something to hold back—a woman, that is. If she just gives the man she loves everything, just like that—"

Vlemk nodded. "I understand." He was thinking, absurd as it may sound, about box-painting, about the risks one ran, the temptations.

"But is it possible?" asked the Princess, "you and I, a box-painter and a Princess?"

"Well, it's *odd* of course," said Vlemk. "No doubt we'll have our critics."

"You won't go back to sleeping in gutters or anything?" the Princess asked.

"I don't think so," said Vlemk, "though life is always full of surprises."

Abruptly forgetting her fears, the Princess reached out her arms to him, smiling joyfully. He bent to her, smiling back, and they embraced, quick and light as children.

Now the servants, having noticed the change in mood around the Princess's bed, crept in nearer to find out what was happening. The Prince too had noticed that everything had changed entirely. "Well," he said, "I must go now, as I said." He made no move to leave.

"You're welcome to stay to supper if you like," the Princess said.

Vlemk, as if the palace were his own, reached out his hand to the Prince. The Prince looked from Vlemk to the Princess. He stood for a long moment staring into space, puzzling things through; then abruptly his face lit up. "No," he said, gripping his cane with a sort of easy firmness, "but I'll come for the wedding. I must go home to my wife."

"And I," said Vlemk, "must go home and make my various preparations."

It was now clear to even the least of the servants that everything had changed and all was well. They seized Vlemk's hands, also the Prince's, kissing the backs and fronts of them and thanking both Vlemk and the Prince for what they'd done. Vlemk beamed, nodding and bowing and telling them on every side, "It's nothing! It's nothing!" moving them along with him to the door as he did so, walking with the Prince, waving his repeated farewells to the picture and the Princess who'd come out to the bedroom door, the box in the Princess's left hand. In the high front room the driver of the carriage was waiting, more elegant than ever, and on either side of him stood servants with armloads of flowers for Vlemk and the Prince. "Come back quickly," cried the Princess and the picture, both at once.

Vlemk waved his hat.

"Well," said the driver, bowing and falling into step beside Vlemk and the Prince, "things have turned out better than I thought they would."

"So they have," said Vlemk. "It's good to have everything settled at last. It's good to know exactly where we stand!"

They came to the high arched door and the driver stepped ahead of Vlemk to seize the door-handle. As he opened the door, a sharp blast of wintery wind swept in, filling out the female servants' skirts like sails and hurling in fine-ground blizzard snow.

"Oh!" cried the Princess and the picture on the box, astonished.

"It's winter!" cried the Prince, so startled he could hardly believe his eyes. Instantly the flowers in the servants' arms began to tremble and wilt, and the leaves of the flowers inside the room began to blow around crazily.

"Winter," said Vlemk, full of wonder, his voice so quiet that only the carriage driver heard.

They had to lift their feet high, Vlemk, the Prince, and the carriage driver, to make it through the drifts to the black-leather, gold-studded carriage. The carriage of the Prince stood just beyond. In every direction except straight above, the world was white and lovely, as if the light came from inside the snow. Straight above — or so it seemed to Vlemk, standing with one hand on his beard, the other in his pocket — the sky was painfully bright, blinding, as if someone had lifted the cover off the world, so that soon, as usual, everything in it would be transformed.

DESIGNED AND PRINTED BY GRANT DAHLSTROM at The Castle Press. The text is set in Linotype Aldus designed by Hermann Zapf. Aldus was named for the 16th-century Venetian printer Aldus Manutius. The paper is Sunray Opaque Vellum.